Our

miniseries has grown!

Now you can share in even more tears and
triumphs as Harlequin Romance®
brings you a month full of

Pregnancy & Proposals, Miracles & Marriage!

Don't miss:

Adopted: Family in a Million
by Barbara McMahon

Hired: Nanny Bride
by Cara Colter

Italian Tycoon, Secret Son
by Lucy Gordon

Blind-Date Baby
by Fiona Harper

The Billionaire's Baby
by Nicola Marsh

Doorstep Daddy
by Shirley Jump

"If I ever had a honeymoon, that's where—"

Dannie broke off, blushing wildly.

If there was one thing a guy as devoted to being single as Joshua did not ever discuss it was weddings. Or honeymoons. But his love of seeing her blush got the better of him.

"What do you mean, if?" he teased her. "If ever toes were made to fit a glass slipper, it's those ones. Some guy is going to fall at your feet and marry you. I'm surprised it hasn't happened already."

"Oh," she said, her voice strangled, even as she tried to act casual. "I've given up Cinderella dreams. Men are mostly cads in sheep's clothing."

"How right you are...."

CARA COLTER
Hired: Nanny Bride

Chicago Public Library
Vodak/East Side Branch
3710 E. 106th St.
Chicago, IL 60617

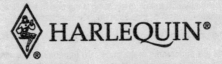

HARLEQUIN®

TORONTO • NEW YORK • LONDON
AMSTERDAM • PARIS • SYDNEY • HAMBURG
STOCKHOLM • ATHENS • TOKYO • MILAN • MADRID
PRAGUE • WARSAW • BUDAPEST • AUCKLAND

If you purchased this book without a cover you should be aware that this book is stolen property. It was reported as "unsold and destroyed" to the publisher, and neither the author nor the publisher has received any payment for this "stripped book."

To Mike Kepke and Aline Pihl
"Love fills a lifetime"
August 9, 2008

Recycling programs
for this product may
not exist in your area.

ISBN-13: 978-0-373-17584-0
ISBN-10:   0-373-17584-1

HIRED: NANNY BRIDE

First North American Publication 2009.

Copyright © 2009 by Cara Colter.

All rights reserved. Except for use in any review, the reproduction or utilization of this work in whole or in part in any form by any electronic, mechanical or other means, now known or hereafter invented, including xerography, photocopying and recording, or in any information storage or retrieval system, is forbidden without the written permission of the publisher, Harlequin Enterprises Limited, 225 Duncan Mill Road, Don Mills, Ontario, Canada M3B 3K9.

This is a work of fiction. Names, characters, places and incidents are either the product of the author's imagination or are used fictitiously, and any resemblance to actual persons, living or dead, business establishments, events or locales is entirely coincidental.

This edition published by arrangement with Harlequin Books S.A.

® and TM are trademarks of the publisher. Trademarks indicated with ® are registered in the United States Patent and Trademark Office, the Canadian Trade Marks Office and in other countries.

www.eHarlequin.com

Printed in U.S.A.

R0421207572

Cara Colter lives on an acreage in British Columbia with her partner, Rob, and eleven horses. She has three grown children and a grandson. She is a recent recipient of a *Romantic Times BOOKreviews* Career Achievement Award in the Love and Laughter category. Cara loves to hear from readers, and you can contact her, or learn more about her, through her Web site, www.cara-colter.com.

Cara Colter brings you another heart-warming Harlequin Romance® novel,

Miss Maple and the Playboy

August 2009

Chicago Public Library
Vodak/East Side Branch
3710 E. 106th St.
Chicago, IL 60617

Dear Reader,

For the past few years I have been helping out in an orchard at harvest time. I do whatever I am asked, from hauling cherries to sorting apples. I come home exhausted, too tired to get groceries, do my banking or cook supper. But I am never too weary to indulge in the luxury of a good story. Reading for pure pleasure is the perfect place to go, more rejuvenating (and less expensive!) than a mud bath at the spa.

I know you, my readers, are real women with real lives. I know you deal with all kinds of pressures, from solo parenting to running companies. I know sometimes you are scared, lonely, bone-tired, buckling under responsibility.

And so I am humbled that the book you are holding right now, in one of those precious and closely guarded free moments, is not just mine, but a romance. It is quite possible that your grandmother and mother also found moments of joy and hope in a book like this, because Harlequin is celebrating a remarkable milestone. It has been honoring what real women like to read by producing these uplifting stories for sixty years. I am proud to be a part of the tradition that gives you the perfect place to go after one of those long, hard days.

Warmest wishes,

Cara Colter

CHAPTER ONE

JOSHUA COLE heard the unfamiliar sound and felt a quiver of pure feeling snake up and down his spine. So rare was that particular sensation that it took him a split second to identify it.

Fear.

He was a man who prided himself on moving forward, rather than back, in any kind of stressful situation. It had turned out to be a strategy for success in the high-powered world he moved in.

Joshua hit the intercom that connected his office to his secretary's desk in the outer lair. His office underscored who he had become with its floor-to-ceiling glass windows that overlooked the spectacular view of Vancouver, downtown skyscrapers in the foreground, majestic white-capped mountains as the backdrop.

But if his surroundings reflected his confidence, at this moment his voice did not. "Tell me that wasn't what I thought it was."

But the sound came again, through his closed, carved, solid walnut door. Now it was amplified by the intercom.

There was absolutely no mistaking it for anything but what it was: a baby crying, the initial hesitant sobs building quickly to strident shrieking.

"They say you are expecting them," said his receptionist, Amber, her own tone rising, in panic or in an effort to be heard above the baby, he couldn't quite be sure.

Of course he was expecting them. Just not today. Not here. Children, and particularly squalling babies, would be as out of place in the corporate offices of the company he had founded as a hippo at Victoria's Empress Hotel's high tea.

Joshua Cole had built his fortune and his company, Sun, around the precise lack of that sound in each of his exclusive adult-only resorts.

His office replicated the atmosphere that made the resorts so successful: tasteful, expensive, luxurious, no detail overlooked. The art was original, the antiques were authentic, the rugs came from the best bazaars in Turkey.

The skillful use of rich colors and subtle, exotic textures made Joshua Cole's office mirror the man, masculine, confident, charismatic. His desk faced a wall that showcased his career rise with beautifully framed magazine covers, *Forbes, Business, Business Weekly.*

But this morning, as always, his surroundings had faded as he intently studied what he hoped would become his next project. The surface of his desk was littered with photos of a rundown resort in the wilderness of the British Columbia interior.

He'd had *that* feeling as soon as he'd seen the photos. Moose Lake Lodge could be turned into an adventure destination for the busy young professionals who trusted his company to give them exactly what they wanted in a vacation experience. His clients demanded grown-up adventure plus five-star meals, spalike luxuries and all against the backdrop of a boutique hotel atmosphere.

The initial overture to Moose Lake Lodge had not gone particularly well. The owners were reluctant to talk to him, let alone sell to him. He had sensed they were wary of his reputation as a playboy, concerned about the effect of a Sun resort in the middle of cottage country. The Moose Lake Lodge had run as a family-oriented lakeside retreat since the 1930s, and the owners had sentimental attachments to it.

But sentiment did not pay the bills, and Joshua Cole did his homework. He knew buyers were not lining up for the place, and he was already strategizing his next move. He would up his offer tantalizingly. He'd convince the Baker family he could turn Moose Lake Lodge into a place they would always feel proud of. He'd visit them personally, win them over. Joshua Cole was very good at winning people over.

And he was passionate about this game, in all its stages: acquiring, renovating, opening, operating.

To that end Joshua had a resort in the Amazon jungle that offered rainforest canopy excursions, and one on the African savannah featuring photo safaris. And, of course, he still had his original small hotel in Italy, in the heart of Tuscany, where it had all started, offering a very grown-up winery and tasting tours.

Most recently Sun had opened a floating five-star destination for water lovers off the Kona Coast, on the Big Island of Hawaii.

Water lovers and kid haters.

Well, not all kid *haters*. Some of his best clients were just busy parents who desperately needed a break from the demands of children.

"WAHHHHH."

As if that sound didn't explain it all. Even his own sister, Melanie, domestic diva that she had become, had accepted his offer to give her and her hubbie a much-needed break at the newly opened Sun in Kona.

No wonder, with a kid whose howls could register off the decibel chart.

How could his niece and nephew be here? His crammed calendar clearly said tomorrow. The plane was arriving at ten in the morning. Joshua planned, out of respect to his sister, to meet the plane, pat his niece on the head and make appropriate noises over the relatively new baby nephew, hopefully without actually touching him. Then he was planning on putting them, and the nanny they were traveling with, in a limo and waving goodbye as they were whisked off to a kid-friendly holiday experience at Whistler.

Holiday for Mom and Dad at the exclusive Kona Sun; holiday for the kids; Uncle Josh, hero-of-the-hour.

The baby screamed nonstop in the outer office, and Joshua's head began to throb. He'd given his sister and brother-in-law, Ryan, the adult-getaway package after the birth of the baby, stunned that his sister, via their Web cam conversations, always so vital in the past, could suddenly look so worn-out. Somehow, he hadn't exactly foreseen *this* moment, though he probably should have when Melanie had started worrying about her kids within seconds of agreeing to go to the Kona Sun for a week. Naturally, her brother, the hero, had volunteered to look after that, too.

He should have remembered that things never went quite as he planned them when his sister was involved.

"What is going on?" Joshua asked in a low voice into his intercom. His legendary confidence abandoned him around children, even ones he was related to.

"There's a, um, woman here. With a baby and another, er, small thing."

"I know *who* they are," Joshua said. "Why is the baby making that noise?"

"You know who they are?" Amber asked, clearly feeling betrayed that they hadn't wandered in off the street, thereby making disposing of them so much easier!

"They aren't supposed to be here. They're supposed to be—

"Miss! Excuse me! You can't just go in there!"

But before Amber could protect him, his office door opened.

For all the noise that baby was making, Joshua was struck by a sudden sensation of quiet as he pressed the off button on the intercom and studied the woman who stood at the doorway to his enclave.

Despite the screaming red-faced baby at her bosom, and his four-year-old niece attached to the hem of her coat, the woman carried herself with a calm dignity, a sturdy sea vessel, innately sure of her abilities in a storm, which, Joshua felt, the screaming baby qualified as.

His niece was looking at him with dark dislike, which took him aback. Like cats, children were adept at attaching themselves to those with an aversion, and he had spent his last visit to his sister's home in Toronto trying to escape his niece's frightening affection. At that time the baby had been an enormous lump under his sister's sweater, and there had been no nanny in residence.

The distraction of the baby and his niece's withering look aside, he was aware of feeling he had not seen a woman like the one who accompanied his niece and nephew for a very long time.

No, Joshua Cole had become blissfully accustomed

to perfection in the opposite sex. His world had become populated with women with thin, gym-sculpted bodies, dentist-whitened teeth, unfurrowed brows, perfect makeup, stunning hair, clothing that *breathed* wealth and assurance.

The woman before him was, in some ways, the epitome of what he expected a nanny to be: fresh-scrubbed; no makeup; sensible shoes; a plain black skirt showing from underneath a hideously rumpled coat. One black stocking had a run in it from knee to ankle. All that was missing was the umbrella.

She was exactly the type of woman he might dismiss without a second look: frumpalumpa, a woman who had given up on herself in favor of her tedious child-watching duties. She was younger than he would have imagined, though, and carried herself with a careful dignity that the clothes did not hide, and that did not allow for easy dismissal.

A locket, gold and fragile, entirely out of keeping with the rest of her outfit, winked at her neck, making him aware of the pure creaminess of her skin.

Then Joshua noticed her hair. Wavy and jet black, it was refreshingly uncolored, caught back with a clip it was slipping free from. The escaped tendrils of hair should have added to her generally unruly appearance, but they didn't. Instead they hinted at something he wasn't seeing. Something wilder, maybe even exotic.

Her eyes, when he met them, underscored that feeling. They were a stunning shade of turquoise, fringed with lashes that didn't need one smidgen of mascara to add to their lushness. Unfortunately, he detected his niece's disapproval mirrored in her nanny's expression.

Her face might, at first glance, be mistaken for plain.

And yet there was something in it—freshness, perhaps—that intrigued.

It was as if, somehow, she was *real* in the world of fantasy that he had so carefully crafted, a world that had rewarded him with riches beyond his wildest dreams, and which suddenly seemed lacking in *something,* and that *something* just as suddenly seemed essential.

He shrugged off the uncharacteristic thoughts, put their intrusion in his perfect world down to the yelps of the baby. He had only to look around himself to know he was the man who already had everything, including the admiration and attention of women a thousand times more polished than the one in front of him.

"My uncle hates us," his niece, Susie, announced just as Joshua was contemplating trying out his most charming smile on the nanny. He was pretty confident he was up to the challenge of melting the faintly contemptuous look from her eyes. Pitting his charm against someone so wholesome would be good practice for when he met with the Bakers about acquiring their beloved Moose Lake Lodge.

"Susie, that was extremely rude," the nanny said. Her voice was husky, low, as real as she was. And it hinted at something tantalizingly sensual below the frumpalumpa exterior.

"Of course I don't hate you," Joshua said, annoyed at being put on the defensive by a child who had plagued him with xoxo notes less than a year ago, explaining to him carefully each x stood for a kiss and each o stood for a hug. "I'm terrified of you. There's a difference."

He tried his smile.

The nanny's lips twitched, her free hand reached up and touched the locket. If a smile had been developing, it never materialized. In fact, Joshua wasn't quite sure if he'd amused her or annoyed her. If he'd amused her, her amusement was reluctant! He was not accustomed to ambiguous reactions when he dealt with the fairer sex.

"You hate us," Susie said firmly. "Why would Mommy and Daddy need a holiday from *us?*"

Then her nose crunched up, her eyes closed tight, she sniffled and buried her face in the folds of the nanny's voluminous jacket and howled. The baby seemed to regard that as a challenge to make himself heard above his sister.

"Why, indeed?" he asked dryly. The children had been in his office approximately thirty seconds, and he already needed a holiday from them.

"She's just tired," the nanny said. "Susie, shush."

He was unwillingly captivated by the hand that she rested lightly on Susie's head, by the exquisite tenderness in that faint touch, by the way her voice calmed the child, who quit howling but hiccupped sadly.

"I think there's a tiny abandonment issue," the nanny said, "that was not in the least helped by your leaving us stranded at the airport."

He found himself hoping that, when he explained there had been a misunderstanding, he would see her without the disapproving furrow in her forehead.

"There seems to have been a mix-up about the dates. If you had called, I would have had someone pick you up."

"I did call." The frown line deepened. "Apparently only very important people are preapproved to speak to you."

He could see how all those security measures intended to protect his time and his privacy were just evidence to her of an overly inflated ego. He was probably going to have to accept that the furrowed brow line would be permanent.

"I'm terribly sorry," he said, which did not soften the look on her face at all.

"Are those women naked?" Susie asked, midhiccup, having removed her head from the folds of her nanny's coat. Unfortunately.

He followed her gaze and sighed inwardly. She was staring at the Lalique bowl that adorned his coffee table. Exquisitely crafted in blue glass, and worth about forty thousand dollars, it was one of several items in the room that he didn't even want his niece to breathe on, though to say so might confirm for the nanny, who already had a low opinion of him, that he really did hate children.

He realized that the bowl, shimmering in the light from the window, was nearly the same shades of blue as the nanny's eyes.

"Susie, that's enough," the nanny said firmly.

"Well, they are naked, Miss Pringy," Susie muttered, unrepentant.

Miss Pringy. A stodgy, solid, librarian spinster kind of name that should have suited her to a T, but didn't.

"In your uncle's circles, I'm sure that bowl would be considered appropriate decor."

"And what circles are those?" Joshua asked, raising an eyebrow at her.

"I had the pleasure of reading all about you on the plane, Mr. Cole. *People to Watch.* You are quite the celebrity it would seem."

Her tone said it all: superficial, playboy, hedonist. Even before he'd missed her at the airport, he'd been tried and found guilty.

Joshua Cole had, unfortunately, been discovered by a world hungry for celebrity, and the fascination with his lifestyle was escalating alarmingly. It meant he was often prejudged, but so far he'd remained confident of his ability to overcome misperceptions.

Though he could already tell that Miss Pringy, of all people, looked as if she was going to be immune to his considerable charisma. He found himself feeling defensive again.

"I'm a businessman," he said shortly, "not a celebrity."

In fact, Joshua Cole disliked almost everything about his newly arising status, but the more he rejected media attention, the more the media hounded him. That article in *People to Watch* had been unauthorized and totally embarrassing.

World's Sexiest Bachelor was a ridiculous title. It perturbed him that the magazine had gotten so many pictures of him, when he felt he'd become quite deft at protecting his privacy.

Where had all those pictures of him with his shirt off come from? Or relaxing, for that matter? Both were rare events.

To look at those pictures, anyone would think he was younger than his thirty years, and also that he spent his days half naked in sand and sunshine, the wind, waves and sun streaking his dark hair to golden brown. The article had waxed poetic about his "buff" build and sea-green eyes. It was enough to make a grown man sick.

Joshua was learning being in the spotlight had a good side: free publicity for Sun for one. For another, the label *playboy* that was frequently attached to him meant he was rarely bothered by women who had apple-pie, picket-fence kind of dreams. No, his constantly shifting lineup of companions were happy with lifestyle-of-the-rich-and-famous outings and expensive trinkets; in other words, no *real* investment on his part.

The downside was that people like the mom-and-pop owners of Moose Lake Lodge weren't comfortable with his notoriety coming to their neck of the woods.

And sometimes, usually when he least expected it, he would be struck with a sensation of loneliness, as if no one truly knew him, though usually a phone call to his sister fixed that pretty quickly!

Maybe it was because the nanny represented his sister's household that he disliked being prejudged by her, that he felt strangely driven to try to make a good impression.

Just underneath that odd desire was an even odder one to know if she was evaluating him as the World's Sexiest Bachelor. If she was, she approved of the title even less than he did. In fact, she looked as if she might want to see the criteria that had won him the title!

Was it possible she didn't find him attractive? That she didn't agree with the magazine's assessment of his status? For a crazy moment he actually cared! He found himself feeling defensive again, saying in his head, *Miss Pringy wouldn't know sexy if it stepped on her.*

Or walked up to her and kissed her.

Which, unfortunately, made him look at her lips. They were pursed in a stern line, which he should have found off-putting. Not challenging! But the tightness around her lips only accentuated how full they were, puffy, *kissable*.

She reached up and touched the locket again, as if it was an amulet and he was a werewolf, as if she was totally aware of his inappropriate assessment of the kissability of her lips and needed to protect herself.

"I'm Danielle Springer, Dannie," the woman announced formally, the woman least likely to have her lips evaluated as kissable. She was still unfazed by the shrill cries of the baby. Again, he couldn't help but notice her voice was husky, as sensuous as a touch. Under different circumstances—very different circumstances—he was pretty sure he would have found it sexy.

At least as sexy as her damned disapproving lips.

"I was told you'd meet us at the plane."

"There seems to have been a mix-up," he said for the second time. "Not uncommon when my sister is involved."

"It's not easy to get children ready for a trip!" She was instantly defensive of her employer, which, under different circumstances, he would have found more admirable.

"That's why you're there to help, isn't it?" he asked mildly.

Her chin lifted and her eyes snapped. "Somehow I am unsurprised that you would think it was just about packing a bag and catching a flight."

She was obviously a woman of spirit, which he found intriguing, so he goaded her a bit. "Isn't it?"

"There's more to raising a child than attending to their physical needs," she said sharply. "And your sister knows that."

"Saint Melanie," he said dryly.

"Meaning?" she asked regally.

"I am constantly on the receiving end of lectures from my dear sister about the state of my emotional bankruptcy," he said pleasantly. "But despite my notoriously cavalier attitudes, I really did think you were arriving tomorrow. I'm sorry. I especially wouldn't want to hurt Susie."

Susie shot him a suspicious look, popped her thumb in her mouth and sucked. Hard.

Dannie juggled the baby from one arm to the other and gently removed Susie's thumb. He could suddenly see that despite the nanny's outward composure, the baby was heavy and Dannie was tired.

Was there slight forgiveness in her eyes, did the stern line around her mouth relax ever so slightly? He studied her and decided he was being optimistic.

He could read what was going to happen before it did, and he shot up from behind his desk, hoping Dannie would get the message and change course. Instead she moved behind the desk with easy confidence, right into his space, and held out the baby.

"Could you? Just for a moment? I think he's in need of a change. I'll just see if I can find his things in my bag."

For a moment, Joshua Cole, self-made billionaire, was completely frozen. He was stunned by the predicament he was in. Before he could brace himself or prepare himself properly in any way, he was holding a squirming, puttylike chunk of humanity.

Joshua shut his eyes against the warmth that crept through him as his eight-month-old nephew, Jake, settled into his arms.

A memory he thought he'd divorced himself from a long, long time ago returned with such force his throat closed.

Bereft.

"Don't worry. It's not what you think," Dannie said. Joshua opened his eyes and saw her looking at him quizzically. "He's just wet. Not, um, you know."

Joshua became aware of a large warm spot soaking through his silk tie and onto his pristine designer shirt. He was happy to let her think his reaction to holding the baby was caused by an incorrect assumption about what Jake was depositing on his shirt.

The baby, as stunned by finding himself in his uncle's arms as his uncle himself, was shocked into sudden blessed silence and regarded him with huge sapphire eyes.

The Buddha-like expression of contentment lasted for a blink. And then the baby frowned. Turned red. Strained. Made a terrifying grunting sound.

"What's wrong with him?" Joshua asked, appalled.

"I'm afraid now it is, um, you know."

If he didn't know, the sudden explosion of odor let the secret out.

"Amber," he called. The man who reacted to stress with aplomb, at least until this moment, said, "Amber, call 911."

Dannie Springer's delectable lips twitched. A twinkle lit the depths of those astonishing eyes. She struggled, lost, started to laugh. And if he hadn't needed 911 before, he did now.

For a time-suspended moment, looking into those amazing blue depths, listening to the brook-clear sound of her laughter, it was as if disaster was not unfolding around him. It was as if his office, last sanctuary of the single male, had not been invaded by the enemy that represented domestic bliss. He might have laughed himself, if he wasn't so close to gagging.

"Amber," he said, trying to regain his legendary control in this situation that seemed to be unraveling dismally, "forget 911."

Amber hovered in the doorway. "What would you like me to do?"

"The children haven't eaten," Miss Pringy said, as if she was in charge. "Do you think you could find us some lunch?"

How could anyone think of lunch at a time like this?

Or put Amber in charge of it? Even though Amber disappeared, Josh was fairly certain food was a question lost on her. As far as Joshua could see, his secretary survived on celery sticks.

Did babies eat celery sticks?

For a moment he felt amazed at how a few seconds could change a man's whole world. If somebody had told him when he walked into his office, he would be asking himself questions about babies and celery sticks before the morning was out, he would not have believed it.

He would particularly not have believed he would be contemplating celery sticks with that odor now permeating every luxurious corner of his office.

But he, of all people, should know. A few seconds could change everything, forever. A baby, wrapped in a blue hospital blanket, his face tiny and wrinkled, his brow furrowed, his tiny, perfect hand—

Stop! Joshua ordered himself.

And yet even as he resented memories of a long-ago hurt being triggered so easily by the babe nestled in his arms now, he was also aware of something else.

He felt surprised by life, for the first time in a very, very long time. He slid his visitor a glance and was painfully aware of how lushly she was curved, as if *she* ate more than celery sticks. In fact, he could picture her digging into spaghetti, eating with robust and unapologetic appetite. The picture was startlingly sensual.

"I'll just change the baby while we wait for lunch."

"In here?" he sputtered.

"Unless you have a designated area in the building?" she said, raising an eyebrow at him.

Joshua could clearly see she was the kind of woman you did not want to surrender control to. In no time flat, she would have the Lalique bowl moved and the change station set up where the bowl had been.

It was time to take control, not to be weakened by his memories but strengthened by them. It was time to put things back on track. The nanny and the children had arrived early. The thought of how his sister would have delighted in his current predicament firmed his resolve to get things to exactly where he had planned them, quickly.

"The washroom is down the hall," Joshua said, collecting himself as best he could with the putty baby trying to insert its pudgy fingers in his nose. "If you'd care to take the baby there, Miss Pringy—"

"Springer—" she reminded him. "Perhaps while I take care of this, you could do something about, er, that?"

A hand fluttered toward the Lalique. He knew it! She was eyeing the table for its diaper changing potential!

"It's art," he said stubbornly.

"Well, it's art the children aren't old enough for."

Precisely one of his many reservations about children. Everything had to be rearranged around them. Naturally, he needed to set her straight. It was his office, his business, his life. No one, but no one, told him how to run it. She and the children were departing as soon as he could arrange the limo and reschedule their reservations by a day.

But when she took the evilly aromatic baby back, after having fished a diaper out of a huge carpetbag she was traveling with, he was so grateful he decided not to set her straight about who the boss was. After she looked after the baby change, there would be plenty of time for that.

Dannie left the room, Susie on her heels. In a gesture

he was not going to consider surrender, Joshua went and retrieved his suit jacket from where it hung on the back of his chair, and gently and protectively draped it over the bowl.

"Thank you," the nanny said primly, noticing as soon as she came back in the room. A cloud of baby-fresh scent entered with her, and Jake was now gurgling joyously.

"Naked is not nice," Susie informed him.

"Well, that depends on—" A look from the nanny made him take a deep breath and change tack. "As soon as we've had some lunch, I'll see to changing the arrangements I've made for you. You'll love Whistler."

"Whistler?" Miss Pringy said. "Melanie never said anything about Whistler. She said we were staying with you."

"I'm not staying with him," Susie huffed. "He hates us. I can tell."

He wondered if he should show her all those little x and o notes, placed carefully in the top drawer of his desk. No, the nanny might see it as a vulnerability. And somehow, as intriguing—and exasperating—as he found her, he had no intention of appearing vulnerable in front of her.

"Don't worry," Joshua told Susie, firmly, "No one is staying with me, because I don't want—"

"Don't you dare finish that sentence," Miss Springer told him in a tight undertone. "Don't you dare."

Well, as if his life was not surprising enough today! He regarded her thoughtfully, tried to remember when the last time anyone had told him what to do was, and came up blank.

And that tone. No one ever dared use that tone on him. Probably not since grade school, anyway.

"Amber," he called.

She appeared at the doorway, looking mutinous, as if one more demand would finish her. "Lunch is on the way up."

"Take the children for a moment. Miss Pringy and I have a few things to say privately."

Amber stared at him astounded. "Take them where?"

"Just your office will do."

Her lips moved soundlessly, like a fish floundering, but then wordlessly she came in and took the baby, holding him out carefully at arm's length.

"You go, too," Miss Pringy said gently to Susie.

It was a mark of her influence on those children, that with one warning look shot at him, Susie traipsed out of the room behind Amber, shutting the door with unnecessary noisiness behind her.

"You weren't going to say you didn't want them in front of them, were you?" Miss Pringy asked, before the door was barely shut.

It bothered him that she knew precisely how he had planned to finish that sentence. It bothered him the way she was looking at him, her gaze solemn and stripping and seemingly becoming less awed by him by the second.

Much as he disliked his fledgling celebrity status, Joshua had to admit he was growing rather accustomed to awe. And admiration. Women *liked* him, and they had thousands of delightful ways of letting him know that.

But no, Miss Pringy looked, well, *disapproving*, again, but then she shook her hair. It was not the flirtatious flick of locks that he was used to, and yet he found himself captivated. He found himself thinking she was really a wild-spirited gypsy dancer disguised, and unpleasantly so, as a straitlaced nanny.

"Look," he said doggedly, "I've made arrangements for you to stay at a lovely resort in Whistler. They organize child activities all day long! Play-Doh sculpture. Movies. Nature walks. I just have to change everything up a day. You should be out of here and on your way in less than an hour."

"No," she said, and shook her hair again. Definitely not flirtatious. She was *aggravated.*

"No?" he repeated, stunned.

"That's not what Melanie told me, and she is, after all, my employer, not you."

Until the moment his sense of betrayal in his sister increased, Joshua had been pleasantly unaware he still harbored it.

His older sister had been with him in those exhilarating early days of the business, but then she'd broken the cardinal rule. It was okay to date the clients; it was not okay to fall head over heels in love with them!

Then she'd decided, after all these years of wholeheartedly endorsing the principles and mission of Sun, that she *wanted* kids.

That was okay. He felt as if he'd forgiven her even though over the past few years it felt as if he had been under siege by her, trying to make him see things her way. His sister had made it her mission to get him to see how great a relationship would be, how miraculous children were, how empty a life without commitment and a relationship and a family was.

She sent him e-mails and cell phone videos of Susie, singing a song, cuddling with her kitty, pirouetting at her ballet classes. Lately, Jake starred in the impromptu productions. The last one had shown him being particularly disgusting in his desperate attempts to hit his own mouth with a steadily deteriorating piece of chocolate cake gripped in his pudgy hands.

Mel's husband, Ryan, a busy and successful building

contractor, a man among men, fearless and macho, was often in the back ground looking practically teary-eyed with pride over the giftedness of his progeny.

For the most part, Joshua had managed to resist his sister's efforts to involve him in her idea of a perfect life. Was the arrival of her children some new twist in her never-ending plot to convince him the life he'd chosen for himself was a sad and lonely place compared to the life she had chosen for herself?

"Why did you invite the children here just to send them away?" Dannie demanded.

"Play-Doh sculpture is nothing to be scoffed at," he insisted.

"We could have done that at home."

"Then why did you come?"

"Melanie had this idea that you were going to spend some time with them."

Joshua snorted.

"She was so delighted that they were going to get to know you better."

"I don't see why," he said.

"Frankly, neither do I!" She sank down on the couch, and he suddenly could see how tired she was. "What a mess. Melanie said I could trust you with the lives of her children. But you couldn't even make it to the airport!"

"She gave me the wrong day!"

"Nothing is more important to your sister than the well-being of Susie and Jake. Surely she couldn't have made a mistake?" This last was said quietly, as if she was thinking out loud.

Joshua Cole heard the doubt in her voice, and he really didn't know whether to be delighted by it or insulted.

"A mistake?" he said smoothly. "Of course not. I said I'd make arrangements for you and the children's accommodations immediately."

Rather than looking properly appreciative, Miss Pringy was getting that formidable look on her face again.

"Mr. Cole," she said sternly, "I'm afraid that won't do."

Joshua Cole lived in a world where he called the shots. "Won't do?" he repeated, incredulous.

"No," she said firmly. "Packing the children off to a hotel in Whistler will not do. That's no kind of a vacation for a child or a baby."

"Well, what is a vacation for them?" he asked. Inwardly he thought, *anything*. If she wanted tickets to Disneyworld, he'd get them. If they wanted to meet a pop star, he'd arrange it. If they wanted to swim with dolphins, he'd find out how to make that happen. No cost was too high, no effort too great.

"They just want to be around people who love them," she said softly. "In a place where they feel safe and cared about. That is what Melanie thought they were coming to or she would never have sent them."

Or gone herself, he thought, and suddenly, unwillingly, he remembered his sister's tired face. No cost was too high? How about the cost of putting himself out?

Had he led Melanie to believe he was finally going to spend some quality time with her kids? He didn't think so. She hadn't really asked for details, and he hadn't provided any. He wasn't responsible for her assumptions.

But Joshua was suddenly very aware that a man could be one of the world's most successful entrepreneurs, moving in a world of power and wealth, controlling an empire, but still feel like a kid around his older sister, still *want* her approval in some secret part of himself.

Or maybe what he wanted was to be worthy of her trust. Something in him whispered, *Be the better man.*

Out loud he heard himself saying, without one ounce of enthusiasm, "I guess they could come stay with me."

Danielle Springer looked, understandably, skeptical of his commitment.

Too late he realized the full ramifications of his invitation.

Miss Pringy, the formidable nanny with the sensual lips and mysterious eyes would be coming to stay with him, too.

And if that wasn't bad enough, he was opening himself up to a world that might have been his, had he hung on instead of letting go of a different baby boy in a lifetime he had left behind himself.

His son.

He wanted to be a better man, worthy of his sister's trust, but who was he kidding? He'd lost faith in himself, in his ability to do the right thing, a long time ago. His sister didn't even know about the college pregnancy of his girlfriend.

He found himself holding his breath, hoping Dannie Springer would not be foolish enough to say yes to his impulsive invitation, wishing he could take it back, before it drew him into places he did not want to go.

"Obviously, we have to stay somewhere for now," she said, her enthusiasm, or lack thereof, matching his exactly. "I'm not subjecting the children to any more travel or uncertainty today."

But his whole world suddenly had a quality of the

uncertain about it. And Joshua Cole did not like it when things in his well-ordered world shifted out of his control. He didn't like it one little bit.

CHAPTER TWO

DANNIE sat in the back seat of the cab, fuming. *The next time I see Melanie, I'm going to kill her,* she decided.

Thinking such a thought felt like a terrible defeat for a woman who prided herself on her steady nature and unflappable calm, at least professionally. To think it toward Melanie showed how truly rattled Dannie was. Melanie, in just a few short months, had become so much more than an employer.

But the truth was that a steady nature was not any kind of defense against a man like Joshua Cole. He was a complete masculine, sexy package, with that brilliant smile, the jade of those eyes, the perfect masculine cut of his facial features, the way he carried himself, the exquisitely expensive clothing over the sleek muscle of a toned body. All of it put together would have been enough to rattle Mother Theresa!

Dannie had known Melanie's brother was attractive. She had seen two pictures of him in the Maynards' home. Not that those pictures could have prepared her for Joshua Cole in the flesh.

Melanie's two framed photos showed her brother through the lens of an ordinary family. Nothing extraordinary about Joshua at twelve, on the beach, scrawny, white, not even a hint of the man he would become. In fact, whatever had been behind that impish grin seemed to be gone from him entirely.

The other picture showed Joshua in a college football uniform, posed, looking annoyingly cocky and confident, again some mischief in him that now seemed to be gone. Though he was undeniably good-looking, that photo showed only a glimmer of the self-possessed man he now was.

"He never finished college," Melanie had said, with a hint of sadness, when she had seen Dannie looking at that picture. For some reason Dannie had assumed that sadness was for her brother's lost potential.

Melanie had seemed to see Joshua as the exasperating kid brother who was an expert at thwarting her every effort to interfere in his life with her wise and well-meaning sisterly guidance. From Melanie's infrequent mentions of her brother, Dannie had thought he managed a hotel or a travel agency, not that he was the president and CEO of one of the world's most up-and-coming companies!

So, the article in *People to Watch* had been a shocker. First, the photos had come a little closer to capturing the pure animal magnetism of the man. The little-boy mischief captured in his sister's snapshots was gone from those amazing smoky-jade eyes, replaced with an intensity that was decidedly sensual.

That sensuality was underscored in the revealing photos of him: muscled, masculine, at ease with his body, oozing a self-certainty that few men would ever master.

Melanie had certainly never indicated her brother was a candidate for the World's Sexiest Bachelor, though his unmarried status seemed to grate on her continually.

Again, the magazine portrayal seemed to be more

accurate than the casual remarks Melanie had tossed out
about him. The magazine described him as powerful,
engaging and lethally charming. And that was just personally. Professionally he was described as driven. The
timing of the openings of his adventure-based adult-
only resorts was seen as brilliant.

In the article, his name had also been paired with
some of the world's wealthiest and most beautiful
women, including actress Monique Belliveau, singer
Carla Kensington and heiress Stephanie Winger-Stone.

By the time he'd stood them up at the airport,
Danielle Springer, the steady one, had already been
feeling nervous about meeting Joshua Cole, World's
Sexiest Bachelor, and had developed a feeling of dislike
for him, just *knowing* he would exude all the superficial
charm and arrogance of a man who had the world
at his feet. He would move through life effort-
lessly, piling up successes, traveling the globe, causing
heartbreaks but never suffering them.

She had already known, before the plane landed,
that Melanie had made a terrible mistake in judgment
sending them all here. That knowledge had only been
underscored by the fact the Great One had not put in an
appearance at the airport, and she had not been able to
penetrate the golden walls that protected him from the
annoyances of real life.

Which begged the question: Why *hadn't* she jumped
at the opportunity to go to Whistler when he had offered
it? It was more than the fact small children and hotels
rarely made a good combination, no matter how "child-
friendly" they claimed to be.

It was more than the fact that the children were exhausted and so was she, not a good time to be making
decisions!

It was that something about him had been unexpected.

He had not been all arrogance and charm. Something ran deeper in him. She had seen it in that unguarded moment when she had thrust Jake upon him, something in his face that said his life had not been without heartbreak, after all.

Stop it, she told herself sternly. They would spend the evening with him. Tomorrow, rested, she would regroup and decide what to do next. The original plan no longer seemed feasible. Spend a week with him? Good grief!

What she was not going to do was call Melanie and Ryan, who needed this time together desperately. At a whisper of trouble, Melanie would come home.

Still, could it really be in the best interests of the children to spend time with their uncle? He'd made it clear he was uncomfortable with children. In fact, his success was based on the creation of a child-free world! There was no sense seeing anything noble in his sudden whim to play the hero and spend time with the niece and nephew he'd invited here in the first place.

And how about herself? How much time could any woman with blood flowing through her veins spend with a man like that without succumbing?

Not, she reminded herself sourly, that there would be anything to *succumb* to. He was rich and powerful and definitely lethally charming. There had been no pictures in the article of him accompanied by women like her.

Women like her: unprocessed, unsophisticated, slightly plump.

She touched the locket on her neck and felt the ache. Only a few weeks ago, the locket would have protected her. *Taken.*

Brent had given it to her before leaving for Europe. "A promise," he'd said, "I will return to you."

Perhaps it would be better to take the locket off, now that it represented a promise broken. On the other hand perhaps it protected her still, reminding her of the fickleness of the human heart, and especially of the fickleness of the *male* human heart.

And besides, she wasn't ready to take it off. She still looked at the photo inside it each night and felt the ache of loss and the stirring of hope that he would realize he had made a mistake....

Though all along maybe the worst mistake had been hers. Believing in what she felt for Brent, even after what she had grown up with. Her own parents' split up had been venomous, their passion had metamorphosed into full-blown hatred that was destructive to all it had touched, including their children. Maybe especially their children.

Thank God, Dannie thought, for the Maynards, for Melanie and Ryan, for Susie and Jake. Thank God she had already been welcomed into the fold of their household when this hurricane of heartbreak had hit her. She would survive because they gave her a sense of family and of belonging, a safe place to fall when her world had fallen apart.

Bonus: loving them didn't involve one little bit of risk!

Though since Brent's call from London, "I'm so sorry, there's someone else," now when Dannie saw the way that Melanie and Ryan looked at each other, she felt a startling stab of envy.

"Hey, lady, are we going somewhere, or are we just sitting here?" the cabbie asked her, waiting for her instructions, impatient.

"When you see the horrible yellow car, follow it," Dannie said. Delivering the variation on the line "Follow that car" gave her absolutely no pleasure.

"A yellow car?" he said, bemused. "Do you think you could be a little more specific?"

Dannie looked over her shoulder. "It's coming now."

The cabbie whistled. "Okay, lady, though in what world a Lamborghini is horrible, I'm not sure."

"Totally unsuited for children's car seats," she informed him. The horrible yellow car, with its horrible gorgeous driver passed them slowly.

A man like that could make a woman rip a locket right off her neck!

She snorted to herself. A man like that could cause a heart to break just by being in the same room, a single glance, green eyes lingering a touch too long on her lips... Joshua's eyes were probably always making promises he had no intention of keeping.

Unattainable to mere mortals, she reminded herself with a sniff. Not that she was a mortal in the market! Done. Brent had finished her. She had given love a chance, nurtured her hopes and dreams over the year he'd been away, *lived* for his cards and notes and e-mails and been betrayed for all her trouble.

Terrible how that vow of being *done* could be rattled so easily by one lingering look from Joshua Cole! How could his gaze have made her wish, after her terrible Brent breakup, that she had not made herself over quite so completely? Gone was the makeup, the fussing over the hair, the colorful wardrobe. On was about fifteen pounds, the result of intensive chocolate therapy!

She was *done,* intent on making herself invisible and therefore safe. How could she possibly feel as if Joshua Cole had *seen* her in a way Brent, whom she had pulled out all the makeover tricks for, never had?

The sports car was so low, she could look in the window and see Jake, his brand-new car seat strapped in securely, facing backward, his black hair standing straight up like dark dandelion fluff.

She refused to soften her view of Joshua Cole because he had insisted on the car seat to get the baby home. Once you softened your view of a man who was lethally charming, you were finished. That's what *lethally* meant.

Besides, there hadn't been enough room in that ridiculous car to put her and Susie to ride with him.

A car like that said a lot about a man. Fast and flashy. Self-centered. Single and planning to stay that way.

Since she was also single and very much planning to stay that way *for the rest of her life, a poor spinster nanny in the basement room*, it was probably unfair to see that as a flaw in him.

Except the car meant he was a *hunter,* on the prowl. Didn't it?

"What does a car like that mean to you?" she asked the cab driver, just in case she had it wrong.

"That you can have any girl you want," he muttered. *Bingo.*

"If he opens her up, I'm not going to be able to keep up with him," the cabbie warned.

"If he opens her up, I'm going to kill him," she said. "He has a baby in there." *My baby.* Of course, Jake was not officially her baby. Unofficially he had won her heart and soul from the first gurgle. Now, post-Brent, she had decided Jake might be the only baby she ever had.

Emotion could capsize her unexpectedly since Brent had hit her with his announcement, and she felt it claw at her throat now, defended against it by telling herself that sweet little baby boy was probably going to be lethally charming someday, just like his uncle.

Twice, in the space of five minutes, steady, dependable Dannie had thought of killing people.

That's what heartbreak did: turned normal, reliable people into bitter survivors, turned them into what they least wanted to be. In fact, it seemed to her, her recent tragedy had the potential to turn her into her parents, who had spent their entire married lives trying to kill each other.

Figuratively. Mostly.

"You shouldn't say you're going to kill people," Susie told her, a confirmation of what Dannie already knew. Susie was hugging the new teddy bear that had arrived in her uncle's office along with the car seat. The teddy bear did not seem to have softened the child's view of her uncle at all.

In Susie's view, Uncle Josh was the villain who had torn her mother away from her. A teddy bear was not going to fix that.

A lesson Uncle Josh no doubt needed to learn! You could not buy back affection.

The car seat and the teddy bear had arrived within minutes of a quiet phone call. Dannie had heard him giving instructions to have a baby crib set up at his apartment. In the guest room with the Jacuzzi. Which begged the question not only how many guest rooms were there, but why did you need a guest room with a Jacuzzi?

Obviously, for the same reason you needed a car like that. Entertaining.

Still, she had gotten the message. He spoke; people jumped.

And he'd better not even think of trying that with her! She might have been the kind of person who jumped before Brent's betrayal. She was no longer!

They arrived at a condominium complex not far from his office building, and Dannie tried very hard not to be awed, even though a guest room with a Jacuzzi should have given her ample time to prepare herself for something spectacular.

She was awed, anyway. Even though Melanie and Ryan certainly had no financial difficulties, she knew she was now moving in an entirely different league.

The high-rise building appeared to be constructed of white marble, glass and water. The landscaping in front of the main door was exquisite: lush grass, exotic flowers, a black onyx fountain shooting up pillars of gurgling foam.

She was fumbling with her wallet when Joshua appeared at the driver's window, baby already on his hip, and paid the driver. He juggled the baby so he could open the door for her. There was no sense noticing his growing comfort with the baby!

Instead, she focused on the fact that if the great Joshua Cole was aware he had parked the horrible yellow thing in a clearly marked no-parking zone, it didn't concern him.

But she'd do well to remember that: rules were for others.

A doorman came out of the building to move the car almost instantly. Another unloaded her luggage from the trunk of the cab.

Joshua greeted both men by name, with a sincere warmth that surprised her. And then he was leading her through a lobby that reminded her of the one and only five-star hotel she had ever stayed at. The lobby had soaring ceilings, deep carpets over marble tile, distressed leather furniture.

For all that, why did it feel as if the most beautiful

thing in the room was that self-assured man carrying a baby, his strength easy, his manner unforced?

Few men, in Dannie's experience, were really comfortable with children. Brent had claimed to like them, but she had noticed he had that condescending, overly enthusiastic way of being around them that children *hated*.

She hoped it was a sign of healing that she had remembered this flaw in her perfect man!

It was a strange irony that, while Joshua Cole had not made any claims about liking children and in fact radiated unapologetic discomfort around them, he was carrying that baby on his hip as if it was the most natural thing in the world to be doing.

Joshua chose that moment to glance down at the bundle in his arms. She caught his look of unguarded tenderness and felt her throat close. Had she just caught a glimpse of something so real about him that it made her question every other judgment she had made?

What if the World's Sexiest Bachelor was a lie? What if the sports car and clothes and office were just a role he'd assumed? What if he was really a man who had been born to be a daddy?

Danger zone, she told herself. What was wrong with her? She had just been terribly disappointed by one man! Why would she be reading such qualities into another that she barely knew?

Besides, there was no doubt exactly why men like Joshua Cole were so successful with women. They had charm down to a science.

It made it so easy to place them in the center of a fantasy, it was so easy to give them a starring role in a dream that she had to convince herself she did not believe in anymore.

Enough of fantasies, she told herself. She had spent the entire year Brent was away building a fantasy around his stupid cards and e-mails, reading into them growing love, when in fact his love had been diminishing. She was a woman pathetic enough to have spent her entire meager savings on a wedding dress on the basis of a vague promise.

Joshua went to a door off the bank of elevators and inserted a key.

The door glided open, and Dannie tried not to gawk at the unbelievable decadence of a private glass elevator. How was a girl supposed to give up on fantasy in a world where fantasy became reality?

The glass-encased elevator eased silently upward, and even Susie forgot to be mad at her uncle and squealed with delight as they glided smoothly higher and higher, the view becoming more panoramic by the second.

The problem with elevators, especially for a woman trying desperately to regain control of suddenly undisciplined thoughts, of her *fantasies,* was that everything was too close in them. She could smell the tantalizing aroma of Joshua, expensive cologne, mixed with soap. His shoulder, enormously broad under the exquisite tailoring of his suit jacket, brushed hers as he turned to let the baby see the view, and she felt a shiver of animal awareness so strong that it shook her to the core.

The reality of being in this elevator with a *real* man made her aware that for a year Brent had not been real at all, but a faraway dream that she could make into anything she wanted him to be.

Had she ever been this aware of Brent? So aware that his scent, the merest brush of his shoulder, could make her dizzy?

She forced her attention to the view, all too aware it had

nothing to do with the rapid beating of her heart. She could see the deep navy blue of an ocean bay. It was dotted with sailboats. Wet-suited sailboarders danced with the white capped waves. Outside of the bay a cruise ship slid by.

All she could think was that she had made a terrible mistake insisting on coming here with him. She touched her locket. *Its* powers to protect seemed measly and inadequate.

To be so *aware* of another human being, even in light of her recent romantic catastrophe, was terrible. To add to how terrible it was, she knew he would not be that aware of her. Since the breakup call, she had stripped herself of makeup, put away her wardrobe of decent clothes, determined to be invisible, to find the comfort of anonymity in her role as the nanny.

The elevator stopped, the doors slid open, and Dannie turned away from the view to enter directly into an apartment. To her left, floor-to-ceiling glass doors that spanned the entire length of the apartment were open to a terraced deck. Exotic flowering plants surrounded dark rattan furniture, the deep cushions upholstered in shades of lime and white. White curtains, so transparent they could only be silk, waved gracefully in the slightly salt-scented breeze.

Inside were long, sleek ultramodern white leather sofas, casually draped with sheepskins. They formed a conversation area around a fireplace framed in stainless steel, the hearth beaded in copper-colored glass tile. The themes of leather, glass and steel repeated themselves, the eye moving naturally from the conversation area to a bar that separated the living area from a kitchen.

The kitchen was magazine-layout perfect, black cabinets and granite countertops, more stainless steel, more copper-colored glass tiles. A wine cooler, state-of-the-art appliances, everything subtle and sexy.

"Don't tell me you cook," she said, the statement coming out more pleading than she wanted.

He laughed. "Does opening wine count?"

Oh, it counted, right up there with the car and the Jacuzzi, as a big strike against him.

Thankfully, it really confirmed what she already knew. She was way out of her league, but vulnerable, too. And the apartment gave her the perfect excuse.

Was he watching her to see her reaction?

"Obviously," she said tightly, "we can't stay here. I'm sorry. I should never have insisted. If you can book us a flight, I need to take the children home."

But the very thought made her want to cry. She told herself it wasn't because his apartment was like something out of a dream, that it called to the part of her that wanted, dearly, to be pampered, that wanted, despite her every effort, to embrace fantasy instead of reject it.

No. She was tired. The children were tired. She couldn't put them all back on a plane today. Maybe tomorrow.

"A motel for tonight," she said wearily. "Tomorrow we can go home."

"What's wrong?"

Everything suddenly seemed wrong. Her whole damned life. She had never wanted anything like the elegance of this apartment, but only because it was beyond the humble dreams she had nurtured for Brent's and her future.

So why did it feel so terrible, a yawning emptiness that could never be filled, that she realized she could never have this? Or a man like him? She hadn't even been able to hold the interest of Brent, pudgy, owlish, *safe*.

Joshua Cole had the baby stuffed under his arm like a football, and was looking at her with what could very easily be mistaken for genuine concern by the hopelessly naive. At least she could thank Brent for that. She wasn't. Hopelessly naive. Anymore.

"Obviously, I can't stay here with the children. They could wreck a place like this in about twenty minutes." The fantasy was about being pampered, enjoying these lush surroundings; the reality was the children wrecking the place and her being frazzled, trying to keep everything in order.

Reality. Fantasy. As long as she could keep the two straight, she should be able to survive this awkward situation.

"That's ridiculous," he said, but uncertainly.

"Dic-u-lous," Susie agreed, her eyes lighting on a pure crystal sculpture of a dolphin in the center of the coffee table.

Dannie took a tighter hold on Susie's hand as the child tried to squirm free. She could already imagine little jam-covered fingerprints on the drapes, crayon marks on the sofas, wine being pulled out of the cooler.

"No," she said. "It's obvious you aren't set up for children. I'd have a nervous breakdown trying to guard all your possessions."

"They're just possessions," he said softly.

Of course he didn't mean that. She'd already seen what he drove. She'd seen him eyeing that bowl in his office with grave concern every time Susie had even glanced in its direction. It was time to call him on it.

"You're less attached to all this than the bowl in your office?" She congratulated herself on just the right tone of disbelief.

"I can move anything that is that breakable."

"Start with the wine," she said, just to give him an idea how big a job it was.

"The cooler locks. I'll do it now." As he moved across the room, he said over his shoulder, "I'll send for some toys as a distraction."

She had to pull herself together. She had to make the best decision for the children. The thought of moving them again, of cooping them up in a hotel room for the night suddenly seemed nearly unbearable.

They would stay here the night. One night. Rested, she would make good decisions tomorrow. Rested, she would be less susceptible to the temptations of his beautiful world. And his drop-dead-gorgeous eyes. And the brilliant wattage of his smile.

Which was directed at her right now. "What kind of toys should I get?" he asked her. He came over and gave her the key to the wine cooler, folded her hand around it.

She desperately wished he had not done that. His touch, warm and strong, filled with confidence, made her more confused about reality and fantasy. How could a simple touch make her feel as if she'd received an electric jolt from fingertip to elbow?

She'd given him an out, but he wasn't taking it. She could see he was the kind of man who made up his mind and then was not swayed.

There was no point in seeing that as admirable. It was mule-stubbornness, nothing more.

"What toys?" he asked her again. He was smiling wickedly, as if he knew the touch of his hand had affected her.

Of course he knew! He radiated the conceited confidence of a man who had played this game with many women. Played. That's why they called them playboys. It was all just a game to him.

"Princess Tasonja!" Susie crowed her toy suggestion. "And the camping play set. I have to have the tent and the backpack. And the dog, Royal Robert." Seeing her uncle look amenable, she added a piece she coveted from a totally different play set. "And the royal wedding carriage. Don't get Jake anything. He's a baby."

He took his cell phone out of his pocket and tried to dial with his thumb while still holding the baby. Apparently, he was going to have someone round up all the toys his niece had demanded.

"I wouldn't bother with Princess Tasonja, if I were you," Dannie managed, in a clipped undertone as Susie slipped free of her hand and skipped over to the sofa where she buried her face in a copper-colored silk pillow. Dannie was pretty sure the remnants of lunch were on that face.

"Why not?"

Why bother telling him that Susie's attention would be held by the Princess Tasonja doll and her entire entourage for about thirty seconds? Why not let him find out on his own that attempts to buy children's affection usually ended miserably? Susie would become a monster of demands once the first one was met.

That was a lesson he probably needed to learn about the car, too. Any woman who would be impressed with such a childish display of wealth was probably not worth knowing.

Her own awed reaction to this apartment probably spoke volumes about her own lack of character!

"I suspect you think it's going to keep her occupied— Susie do not touch the dolphin. But it won't. Unless you are interested in playing princess doll dress up with her, the appeal will be strictly limited."

He clicked the cell phone shut. "What do I do with her if I don't buy her toys?" he asked.

"You are a sad man," she blurted out, and then blushed at her own audacity.

"I don't do kids well. That doesn't make me *sad*." He regarded her thoughtfully and for way too long.

Swooning length.

"You don't just work for my sister," he guessed. "You hang out with her, sharing ideas. Scary. I'm surprised she doesn't have you married off." He looked suddenly suspicious. "Unless that's why you're here."

"Excuse me?"

"My sister has been on this 'decent girl' kick for a while. She better not be matchmaking."

"Me?" Dannie squeaked. "You?" But suddenly she had a rather sickening memory of Melanie looking at her so sadly as she'd dealt with her news about Brent, as if everyone had expected it *except* her.

Joshua's look grew very dark. "Do you have a boyfriend?"

"Not at the moment," she said coolly, as if she'd had dozens of them, when she'd had only one serious relationship, and the greatest part of that had been by long distance. "But you needn't worry, Mr. Cole. Your sister would know me well enough to know that you are not my type!"

He had the nerve to look offended, as if he just naturally assumed he was every woman's type, the title of World's Sexiest Bachelor obviously having gone straight to his handsome head. "Really? And what is your type?"

She could feel heat staining her cheeks to a color she just knew would be the most unflattering shade of red ever. "Not you!"

"That isn't really an answer."

"Studious, serious about life, not necessarily a sharp

dresser, certainly not materialistic." She was speaking too fast, and in her panic describing a man she knew was less than ideal to a T.

"Priests aren't generally available," he said dryly.

"I meant someone like a college professor." Which was what Brent had been. Rumpled. Academic. Faintly preoccupied all the time. Which she had thought was adorable!

"Your ideal man is a college professor?"

"Yes!" How dare he say it with such scorn?

"Miss Dannie Springer, don't ever take up poker. You can't lie. You're terrible at it."

"As it happens, I don't like poker, and neither does my ideal man." With whom her whole relationship, in retrospect, had been a lie, concocted entirely by her, sitting at home by herself making up a man who had never existed.

"The college professor," he said dryly.

"Yes! Now, if you'll entertain Susie for a bit, it's time for Jake to have a bath." Of course, it wasn't anywhere near time Jake had a bath, but she had to get out of this room and this conversation. She doubted Mr. Playboy of the World knew anything about baby bath times. Or college professors for that matter! But he seemed to know just a little too much about women, and his look was piercing.

"Entertain Susie?" he said, distracted just as she had hoped. "How? Since you've nixed Princess Tasonja."

"Try noughts and crosses."

He frowned. "Like those notes she used to give me? Before she hated me? That were covered with x's and o's that meant hugs and kisses?"

Dannie steeled herself. He was not *really* distressed that he had fallen into his niece's disfavor. His world was way too big that he could be brought down by the little things.

"Noughts and crosses," she said. "Tic-tac-toe."

He looked baffled, underscoring how very far apart their worlds were, and always would be.

"Get a piece of paper and a pencil, Susie will be happy to show you how it works," she said.

"You mean a piece of paper and a pencil will keep her as entertained as the princess?"

"More."

"Do I let her win?" he asked in a whisper. He shot his niece a worried look.

"Would that be honest?"

"For God's sake, I'm not interested in honest."

"I'm sure truer words were never spoken," she said meanly, getting back at him for being so scornful of her college professor.

"I'm interested in not making a little girl cry."

"It's about spending time with her. That's the important part. Not winning or losing."

"I have a lot to learn."

"Yes, you do, Mr. Cole," she said, aware of a snippy little edge to her voice.

"You have a lot to learn, too," he said, quietly, looking at her with an unsettling intensity that she would have done anything to escape.

"Such as?" she said, holding her ground even though she wanted to bolt.

"The college professor. Not for you."

"How would you know?"

"I'm an astute judge of people."

"You aren't! You didn't even know whether or not to be honest playing noughts and crosses."

"Not miniature people, the under-five set. But you,

I know something about you. I wonder if you even know it yourself."

"You know nothing about me that I don't know about myself!" she said recklessly. To her detriment, part of her wanted to hear what he had to say. How often, after all, did an invisible nanny get to hear love advice from the World's Sexiest Bachelor?

But he didn't say a word, just proved exactly why he was the World's Sexiest Bachelor. He lifted her chin with the tip of his finger and looked deep into her eyes. Then he touched her lip with his thumb.

If it was possible to melt she would have. She felt like chocolate exposed to flame. She felt every single lie she had ever told herself about Brent. Dannie yanked away from him, but he nodded, satisfied that he did know something she didn't know herself.

Except now she had an idea.

That she was as weak as every other damn woman he'd ever met. Not that he ever had to know that!

"You're in the bedroom at the end of the hall," he said, as if he hadn't shaken her right to the core. "I had the crib set up in there. Is that okay?"

"Perfect," she said tightly, and she meant it. A pint-size chaperone for weaklings, not that she needed to worry about this man sneaking into her room in the dead of night. That was fantasy.

Of the X-rated variety, and she didn't mean tic-tac-toe, either.

"Hey, Susie," he said turning from her, after one last look that seemed more troubled than triumphant, "do you want to play noughts and crosses?"

Susie glared at him, clearly torn between personal dislike and the temptation of her favorite game. "All right," she said grudgingly.

Danielle marched down the hall with the baby. The room at the end had the same spectacular views and windows as the rest of the apartment.

The decorating was so romantic it was decadent, the whole room done in shades of brown, except for the bed linens that were seductively and lushly cream colored, inviting in that sea of rich dark chocolate.

Her suitcases were on the bed. How that had happened she wasn't quite sure. A crib had been set up for Jake, too.

Through a closed door was a bathroom, with the Jacuzzi.

A jetted tub built for two.

"We have to get out of here," she confided in the baby as she took his plump, dimpled limbs out of his clothes. The fact that Joshua thought his sister might be match-making—and that she could not say with one hundred per cent certainty that Melanie was not—just added an element of humiliation to the urgency she felt to go.

Was Melanie matchmaking? She frowned, thinking back over her conversations with her employer. As eager as Mel was to have everyone in the world enjoy the same state of wedded bliss she lived in, she had always been reserved about Brent.

Dannie assumed because she had never met him.

She had assumed Mel's eagerness to have her join her children with their uncle had only been her effort to help her nanny over her heartbreak, to give her a change of scenery. A hidden agenda? Wouldn't that be humiliating?

But Mel had never alluded, even subtly, to the pos-sibility she considered her nanny and her brother to be anything of a match.

Because we so obviously are not, Dannie thought, and detected just a trace of sulkiness in that conclusion.

As always, the baby worked his magic on her sour mood, her tendency toward dour introspection. Dannie put about two inches of water in the gigantic tub, and Jake surrendered his little naked self gleefully into the watery playpen.

When the baby began to laugh out loud, she was drawn in, and she laughed back, splashing his little round tummy with warm water until he was nearly hysterical with joy.

"Do I take myself and life way too seriously, Mr. Jake?"

What if Mel *had* sent her here with some kind of hidden agenda? So what? What if she just played along?

"Oh, Dannie," she chided herself, "that would be like playing patty-cake with a powder keg."

Jake recognized the term, cooperatively held out his hands and crowed.

Relax, she ordered herself. *If you still know how,* and then sadly, *if you ever knew how.*

CHAPTER THREE

"PATTY cake, patty cake, baker's man, bake me a cake as fast as you can."

Dannie's voice and her laughter, intermingled with happy shouts from the baby and splashing noises, floated down the hallway to where Joshua sat opposite Susie on the couch.

Who would have imagined the serious, rather uptight nanny could sound like that? So intriguingly carefree?

Not that that was the truth about her. No, the truth was what he had *felt* when he had touched her lip—

"Tic, tac, toe," Susie cried and drew a triumphant line though her row of crosses.

Susie was trouncing him at noughts and crosses.

Something unexpected was happening to him. Given that his carefully executed schedule had gone out the window, he felt unexpectedly relaxed, as if a tightly wound coil inside of him was unwinding. Watching his niece, whose tongue was caught between her teeth in fierce concentration, listening to Dannie and the baby, he felt a *feeling* unfurling inside him.

It couldn't possibly be yearning.

He had the life every man worked toward, success beyond his wildest dreams, the great car, the fabulous apartment, gorgeous women as abundant in his life as apples on a tree. Just as ready to be picked, too.

And yet all of that paled in comparison to a baby's laughter and a little girl playing noughts and crosses. All that paled in comparison to the softness of a woman's lip beneath his thumb.

His sister, diabolical schemer that she was, would be thrilled by this turn of events.

What had he been thinking when he had touched Dannie's lip? When he had said to her with such ridiculous confidence, "I know something about you. I wonder if you even know it yourself."

The truth was he hadn't been thinking at all. Thinking belonged to that other world: of deals, successes, planning. That other world of accumulating more and more of the stuff.

The stuff that had failed to make him feel as full as he felt in this moment.

No, the truth was that thought had abandoned him when he touched her. Something deeper had temporarily possessed him.

He had seen her, not through his mind, but with his heart. He had seen her and *felt* the lie she had told him about the college professor. How could she even kid herself that she would ever be happy with a staid life?

From the second she had appeared in his office, she had presented the perfect picture of a nanny. Calm, controlled, prissy.

And from the beginning, he had seen something else. A gypsy soul, wanting to dance. That is what he knew about her that she did not know about herself.

That the right man—and probably not a college professor—was going to make her wild. Would make her toss out everything she thought she believed about herself. Under that costume of respectability she wore beat the drum of passion.

Stop, he told himself. *What is wrong with me?*

"I win," Susie said, carefully checking the placement of her crosses. "Again. You're dumb."

He stared at her, and then started to laugh. Yesterday he would have disagreed, probably argued, but today, since he had done one extremely dumb thing after another, starting with inviting them here, and ending with touching Dannie Springer's most delectable lip, he knew Susie was right.

"Let this be a lesson to you," he said. "Don't drop out of school."

"I don't even go to school yet," Susie informed him. "But when I do, I will love it. I will never ever stop going. I will go to school until I am one hundred."

That was precisely how he had felt about college. From the first day, he'd had a sense of arrival. This was where he belonged. He loved learning things. He loved playing football. He loved the girls, the parties, all of it.

And then, in his senior year, along came Sarah. They were "the" couple on campus. The cool ones. The ones everyone wanted to be. She played queen to his king. Looking back, something he rarely did, what they had called love seemed ridiculously superficial.

And in the end it had been. It had not stood up to the test life had thrown at it. Despite the fact they had taken every precaution, Sarah was pregnant.

Funny how, when he'd found out, he'd felt a rush, not of fear, but of excitement. He'd been willing to do whatever it took to give his baby a family, a good life.

Sarah had been stunned by his enthusiasm. "I'm not keeping it."

To this day, he could feel the bitterness, a force so real and so strong, he could nearly taste it on his tongue, when he remembered those words and the look on her face when she'd said them. "It."

He'd actually, briefly and desperately, considered keeping the baby himself. But reality had set in, and reluctantly he had gone along with Sarah. He'd stuck with her through the pregnancy and the birth.

It was a boy.

And then he'd made the mistake.

He'd held his son in his arms. He had felt the incredible surge of love and protectiveness. He had felt that moment of connection so intense that it seemed nothing else in his life but that moment had ever mattered.

He had known, *I was born to do this.*

But it was too late. He'd held his baby, his son, his light, for about five minutes. And then he'd let go. He had not met the adoptive parents.

Every other reality had faded after that. Nothing mattered to him, not school, not life, not anything at all. His grief was real and debilitating.

Sarah, on the other hand, had chosen not to see the baby, and she moved on eagerly, as if nothing had happened. He was part of what she left behind, but really, he had continued with her throughout the pregnancy out of a sense of honor and decency. But he had never forgiven her the "it."

He dropped out of college a month before he was supposed to graduate, packed a backpack, bought a ticket to anywhere. He'd traveled. Over time, he had come to dislike going to places with children. The sound of their laughter, their energy, reminded him of what he was supposed to be and was not.

When he'd come across Sarah's obituary a few years ago, killed in a ski accident in Switzerland, he had taken his lack of emotion as a sign he'd been a man unworthy of raising that child, anyway.

"Are you all right?"

He hadn't seen her come down the hallway, but now Dannie was standing in the doorway, Jake wrapped up in a pure white towel, only his round, rosy face peeking out, and a few spikes of dark hair.

Her blouse was soaked, showing off full, lush curves, and she looked as rosy as the baby.

Dannie looked at home with Jake, comfortable with her life. Why was she content to raise other people's children, when she looked as if she'd been born to hold freshly bathed babies of her own?

"All right?" he stammered, getting up from the couch. "Yeah. Of course."

But he wasn't. He was acutely aware that being around these kids, around Dannie, was making him feel things he had been content not to feel, revisit places he had been relieved to leave behind.

All he had to do was get through the rest of tonight. Tomorrow he'd figure out how to get rid of them, or maybe she would decide to go.

That would be best for everyone involved, and to hell with his sister's disapproval.

Though what if Mel cut her own vacation short? She needed it.

"Are you sure you're all right?" Dannie asked, frowning.

He pulled himself together, vowed he was not going back to the memory of holding his baby. He could not revisit the pain of letting that little guy go and survive. He couldn't.

He was going to focus totally and intensely on this moment.

He said, with forced cheer, "As all right as a guy can be whose been beaten at noughts and crosses by a four-year-old, thirty-three times in a row."

Because of his vow to focus on the moment, he became acutely aware of what it held. Dannie. Her hair was curling from the moistness, her cheeks were on fire, her blouse was sticking to her in all the right places.

He glanced at Susie, who was drawing a picture on the back of a used piece of paper, bored with the lack of competition.

Her picture showed a mommy, a daddy, a child suspended between their stick arms, big smiles on their oversize heads.

Despite his vow, the thought hit him like a slug. The world he had walked away from.

His son would have been three years older than his niece. Did he look like Susie? Worse, did he look like him?

He swore under his breath, running a hand through his hair.

"Mr. Cole!"

Susie snickered, delighted at the tone of voice he'd earned from her nanny.

"Sorry," he muttered, "Let's go get something to eat." His mind wandered to the thought of Danielle eating spaghetti. "There's a great Italian restaurant around the corner. Five-star."

Dannie rolled her eyes. "Have you ever taken a baby and a four-year-old to a restaurant?"

No, he wanted to scream at her, *because I walked away from that life.*

"So, we'll order pizza," he snapped.

"Pizza," Susie breathed, "my favorite."

"Pizza, small children and white leather. Hmm," Dannie said.

"I don't care about the goddamned leather!" he said.

He expected another reprimand, but she was looking at him closely, way too closely. Just as he had seen things about her that she might have been unaware of, he got the same feeling she saw things like that about him.

"Pizza sounds great," she said soothingly.

Glad to be able to move away from her, to take charge, even of something so simple, he went and got a menu out of the drawer by the phone.

"What kind?" he asked.

"Cheese," Susie told him.

"Just cheese?"

"I hate everything else."

"And what about you, Miss Pringy? Can we order an adult pizza for us? The works?"

"Does that include anchovies?"

"It does."

"I think I'm in heaven," she said.

He looked at her wet shirt, the beautiful swelling roundness of a real woman. He thought maybe he could be in heaven, too, if he let himself go there. But he wasn't going to.

She glanced down at where he was looking and turned bright, bright red. She waltzed across the space between them, and placed the towel-wrapped baby in his arms.

"I need to go put on something dry."

The baby was warm, the towel slightly damp. A smell tickled his nostrils: something so pure it stung his eyes.

He realized he'd had no idea what heaven was until

that moment. He realized the survival of his world probably depended on getting these children, and her, back out of his life.

She wanted to go. He wanted her to go.

So what was the problem?

The problem was, he suspected, both of them knew what they wanted, and neither of them knew what they needed.

Dannie reemerged just as the pizza was brought to the front desk. She was dressed casually, in black yoga pants and a matching hoodie, which, he suspected, was intended to hide her assets, and which did nothing of the sort. Her figure, minus the ugly black skirt, was amazing, lush.

Her complexion was still rosy from the bath. Or she was blushing under his frank look.

He had to remember she was not the kind of woman he'd become accustomed to. Sophisticated. Experienced. *Expecting* male admiration.

"I'll just run down to the lobby and pick up the pizzas," he said. He glanced at her feet. They were bare, each toenail painted hot, exotic pink.

He turned away quickly. College professor, indeed! He'd *known* that's what she was hiding. What he hadn't known was how he, a man who spent time with women who were quite comfortable sunbathing topless, would find her naked toes so appealing.

Would have a sudden vision of chasing her through this apartment until she was breathless with laughter.

What would he do with her when he caught her?

He almost said the swear word out loud again. Instead he spun on his heel and took the elevator down to the lobby. He took his time getting back, cooling down, trying to talk sense to himself.

He might as well not have bothered. When he returned to the apartment, she was in the kitchen, scowling at his fridge.

"This is pathetic," she told him.

"I know." He brushed by her and set the pizza down. He tried not to look at her feet, snuck a peek, felt a funny rush, the kind he used to feel a long time ago, in high school, when Mary Beth McKay, two grades older than him, had smiled at him.

It was obviously a lust for the unobtainable.

She was studying his fridge. "No milk. No juice. No ketchup."

"Ketchup on pizza?" he asked.

"I'm just making a point."

"Which is?"

"Your fridge is empty." But it sounded more like she had said his life was empty.

Ridiculous. His life was full to overflowing. He worked twelve-hour days regularly and sixteen-hour days often. His life was filled with constant meetings, international travel, thousands of decisions that could be made only by him.

His life was million-dollar resorts and grand openings. The livelihoods of hundreds of people depended on him doing his work well. His life was flashy cars and flashier women, good restaurants, the fast lane. So why was he taking her disapproving inventory of his fridge as an indictment?

"Do you have peanut butter?" she asked, closing the fridge and opening a cabinet.

"On pizza?" he asked, a bit defensively. "Or are you making a point again?"

"Just thinking ahead," she said. "Breakfast, lunch." She took a sudden interest in a sack of gourmet coffee, took it out and read the label. "Until you make arrangements for us to go. Which you probably will, immediately after you've seen the children eat pizza."

"Give me some credit," he said, though of course that was exactly what he wanted to do. Feed them pizza, talk to his assistant who made all his travel arrangements, get them gone. "Do you want wine? As you've seen, my beverage choices are limited."

"No, thank you," she said. *Primly.*

Good for her. A glass of wine would be the wrong thing to add to the mix. Especially for her. She'd probably get drunk on a whiff of the cork.

They had no high chair, so he held the baby on his lap and fed him tidbits of crust and cheese. She'd been right about the mess. Despite his efforts, Jake looked as if he'd been cooked inside the pizza.

His cell phone rang during dinner, Susie, her lips ringed in bright-red tomato sauce, scowled at him when he fished it out of his pocket.

"My Daddy doesn't answer his phone when we eat," she informed him.

"I'm not—" he swallowed *your daddy* at the warning look on Miss Pringy's face and shut his phone off "—going to, either, then."

When was the last time he'd done anything for approval? But there was something about the way those two females were beaming at him that made him think he'd better get back in the driver's seat. Soon.

Maybe after supper.

Immediately, whoever had tried his cell phone tried his landline. The answering machine picked up.

"Mr. Cole, it's Michael Baker. If you could get back to me as soon as—"

He practically tossed the tomato-sauce stained baby

to Dannie. Susie, noticing the nanny's hands were full, decided she had to have a pencil, right then. She jumped up from her seat.

"No," Dannie called. "Susie, watch your hands."

But it was too late. A pizza handprint decorated his white sofa.

"Michael," he said to the owner of Moose Lake Lodge, "good to hear from you."

Susie was staring at the pizza smudge on his couch. She picked up the hem of her shirt and tried to wipe it off. Out of the corner of her eye, she saw Dannie moving toward her.

"I can fix it myself!" she screamed. "I didn't mean to."

"Just a sec," he put the phone close to his chest. "It's nothing," he told the little girl. "Forget it."

But Susie had decided it was something. Or something was something. She began to howl. Every time Dannie got near her, she darted away, screaming and spreading tomato sauce disaster. Dannie, encumbered by the baby, didn't have a hope of catching her.

"Sorry," he said into the phone. How could one little girl make it sound like World War III was occurring? How could one little girl be spreading a gallon of pizza sauce when he could have sworn the pizza contained a few tablespoons of it at the most? The baby, focused on his sister, started to cry, too. Loudly.

He was going to take the phone and disappear into his den with it, but somehow he couldn't leave Dannie to deal with this mess. He sighed.

Regretfully he said, "I'll have to call you back. A few minutes."

He went and took the baby back from Dannie, and sat on the couch, never mind that the baby was like a pizza sauce squeeze bottle. His shirt was pretty much toast, anyway.

"I want my mommy," Susie screamed. And then again, as if he might have missed the message the first time. "I want my mommy!"

He didn't know where the words came from.

He said, "Of course you want your mommy, honey." He probably spoke with such sincerity because he dearly wanted her mommy right now, too. Here, not soaking up the sun in Kona, but right here, guiding him through this sticky situation.

Something in his voice, probably the sincerity, stopped Susie midhowl. She stared at him, and then she came and sat on the couch beside him.

He held his breath. The baby took his cue from his sister, quieted, watched her intently, deciding what his next move would be.

Susie leaned her head on Joshua's arm, sighed, popped her thumb in her mouth, and the room was suddenly silent except for the sound of her breathing, which became deeper and deeper. Her eyes fluttered, popped open and then fell shut again. This time they didn't reopen.

The baby regarded his sleeping sister, sighed, burrowed into his uncle's chest and slept, too.

"What was that?" Joshua whispered to Dannie.

"Two very tired kids," she said. "Susie has been acting up a bit ever since she heard her parents were planning a vacation that did not include her."

His fault. Sometimes even when a guy had the best of intentions, things went drastically wrong.

"I'm sorry," he said.

"I actually think it's good for them to experience a little separation now and then. It'll help them figure out the world doesn't end if Mel and Ryan go away."

"What now?" he said.

"Well, if you don't mind a few more pizza stains, I suggest we just pop them into their beds. I can clean them up in the morning."

She held out her arms for the baby, who snored solidly through the transfer. Then he picked up his niece.

Who was just a little younger than his son would be.

And for the first time in his life, he put a child to bed. Tucked clean sheets around little Susie, so tiny in sleep. So vulnerable.

Who was tucking his son in tonight? Was the family who adopted him good enough? Kind? Decent? Fun-loving? People with old-fashioned values and virtues?

These were the thoughts he hated having, that he could outrun if he kept busy enough, if he never let himself get too tired or have too many drinks.

He left Susie's room as if his feet were on fire, bumped into Dannie in the hall outside her room where she had just settled Jake.

"Are you okay?" she asked.

"Oh. Sure. Fine. Why wouldn't I be okay?"

She regarded him with those huge blue eyes, the eyes that *expected* honesty, and he had the feeling if you spent enough time around someone like her, you wouldn't be able to keep the mask up that kept people out.

"You just look," she tilted her head, studied him, "as if you've seen a ghost."

A ghost. Not quite.

"A kind of a ghost," he said, forcing lightness into his tone. "I'm remembering what my home looked like before pizza."

She smiled. "I tried to warn you. I'll have it cleaned up in a jiff."

"No, we'll clean it up." In a jiff. Who said things like that? Probably people with old-fashioned values and virtues.

A little later he tossed a damp dishcloth in the sink. He was a man who had trekked in Africa and spelunked in Peru. He had snorkeled off the coast of Kona and bungee jumped off the New River Gorge Bridge in West Virginia.

How was it something so simple—tracking down all the stains and moving all the items that were delicate and breakable—seemed oddly *fun,* as if he was fully engaged, fully alive for the first time in a long time?

Is that what a woman like her would make life like? Fun when you least expected it? Engaging without any trinkets or toys?

Was it time to find out?

"Do you want that glass of wine now?" he asked her, when she threw a tomato-sauce-covered rag into the sink beside his. "You're off duty, aren't you?"

"I'm never off duty," she said, but not sanctimoniously. Still, she was treating the offer with caution.

Which was smart. As his niece had pointed out to him earlier, he wasn't smart. Plain old dumb.

"It's more than a job for you, isn't it?" he asked, even though he knew he should just let her get away to do whatever nannies did once the kids were asleep.

She blinked, nodded, looked away and then said in a low, husky voice, filled with reverence, "I love them."

He felt her words as much as heard them. He felt the sacredness of her bond with his niece and nephew and knew how lucky his sister was to have found this woman.

But how had it happened that Dannie loved the children enough, apparently, to put her own college-professor dreams on hold, her own dreams for her life, her own ambitions?

He wanted to say something, and he didn't. He didn't want to know anymore about what she was giving up for other people's children.

"I think we should go tomorrow," she said, taking a deep breath. "I know your intentions are good, but the children really need to be someplace where they can romp. Someplace not so highly vulnerable to small hands, pizza sauce, the other daily catastrophes of all that energy."

Her eyes said, *I need to be away from you.*

And he needed to be away from her. *Fast.* Before he asked more questions that would reveal to him a depth of love that shone like water in a desert, beckoning, calling.

"I'll go make the arrangements," he said coolly. "I have to return a phone call, anyway."

"I'll say good-night, then, and talk to you in the morning."

He nodded, noticing she did not go back to her room but slipped out onto the terrace. He watched her for a moment as she stood looking out at darkness broken by lights reflecting in the water, stars winking on overhead. The sea breeze picked up her hair, and he yearned to stand beside her, immerse himself in one more simple moment with her.

Moments, he reminded himself harshly, that were bringing up memories and thoughts he didn't want to deal with.

Unaware she was being watched, she turned slightly. He saw her lift the chain from around her neck, open the locket and look at it.

There was no mistaking, from the look on her face, that she had memories of her own to deal with. And he didn't want to know what they were!

He walked away from the open patio doors, and

moments later he shut the door of his home office. He waited for the familiar surroundings to act as a balm on him, to draw him back into his own world.

But they didn't. He thought of her standing on the deck with the wind lifting her hair. The fact that he suddenly didn't want her to go was all the more reason to make the arrangements immediately. Thinking of them leaving filled him with relief. And regret. In nearly equal proportions.

He glanced at his watch. It had been less than eight hours since she had arrived in his office.

His whole world had been turned topsy-turvy. He had revisited a past he thought was well behind him. He was feeling uncertainties he didn't want to feel.

He needed the safety and comfort of his own world back.

He dialed Michael Baker's number.

Michael sounded less guarded than he had in the past, almost jovial.

"It sounded like you had your hands full," he said to Joshua.

"My niece and nephew are here for a visit."

"My wife and I were under the impression you didn't like children," Michael said.

"Don't believe everything you read," Joshua said carefully, sensing the slightest opening of a door that had been firmly closed.

"We had decided to just tell you no," Michael said. "Moose Lake Lodge is not at all like any of your other resorts."

Baker said that in a different way than he had said it before, in a way that left Joshua thinking the door was open again. Just a little bit. Just enough for a shrewd salesman to slip his foot in.

"None of my resorts are ever anything like the other ones. They're all unique."

"This is a family resort. We're kind of hoping it always will be. Does that fit into your plans?"

To just say *no* would close the door irrevocably. He needed to meet with the Bakers. He needed them to trust and like him. He was certain he could make them see his vision for Moose Lake Lodge. Hikes. Canoe and kayak adventures. Rock climbing. The old retreat alive with activity and energy and excitement.

Whether that vision held children or not—it didn't— was not something Joshua felt he had to reveal right now.

"I could fly up tomorrow," Joshua said. "Just meet with me. I'm not quite the superficial cad the press makes me out to be. We'll talk. You don't have to agree to anything."

"You might be making the trip for nothing."

"I'm willing to risk it. I'd love to see it. It's a beautiful place in the pictures." He always did his homework. "Just being able to have a look at the lodge would be great. I understand your grandfather logged the trees for it and built it nearly single-handedly, with a block and tackle."

Hesitation. "Maybe we have been hasty in our judgments. We really don't know anything about you."

"No, you don't."

"It probably couldn't hurt to talk."

"That's how I feel."

"No lawyers, though. No team. Unless—"

"Unless what?"

"How long are your niece and nephew with you?"

A few more hours. "It hasn't quite been decided."

"Look, why don't you bring them up for a few days? Sally and I will get to know you, and a little about your plans for Moose Lake. The kids can enjoy the place. This is the first year we haven't booked in families, because we're trying to sell and we didn't want to disappoint anyone if it sold. We're missing the sound of kids."

It was an answer to a prayer, really, though how anybody could miss the sound that had just filled his apartment, Joshua wasn't quite sure.

Still, the situation was shaping up to be win-win. He could give the kids the vacation he'd promised his sister. He could woo the owners of the Moose Lake Lodge.

It occurred to him he should ask the nanny if she thought the trip would be in the kids' best interests, but she had a way of doing the unpredictable, and she probably had not the least bit of concern in forwarding his business concerns.

She might even see it as using the children.

Was he using the children?

The little devil that sat on every man's shoulder, that poked him with its pitchfork and clouded his motives, told him of course not!

Told him he did not have to consult the nanny. He was the children's uncle! Susie had wanted a camping toy. This was even better! A real camping experience.

"We'll be there tomorrow," he said smoothly. "I'll land at the strip beside the lake around one." He was juggling his schedule in his head. "Would two days be too much of an inconvenience?"

"Two days? You mean fly in one day, and leave the next? That's hardly worth the trip. Why don't you make it four?"

He couldn't make it four. His schedule was impossible to squeeze four days out of. On the other hand, if he stayed four days, he could send the kids home knowing their mother and father would be only a day or two behind them. He could claim he had given them a real holiday.

Plus he could have four whole days to convince the Bakers that their lodge would be safe in the hands of Sun.

"Four days," he agreed smoothly. "It sounds perfect."

"We'll be at the runway to pick you up."

Joshua put down the phone and regarded it thoughtfully. The usual excitement he felt as he moved closer to closing a deal was strangely absent. Somehow he thought maybe he had just created more problems than he had solved.

CHAPTER FOUR

DANNIE woke up and stretched luxuriously. The bed was phenomenal, the linens absolutely decadent. She snuggled deeper under the down comforter, strangely content, until she remembered the day held nothing but uncertainty.

Had Joshua booked them tickets for home? Why did she feel sad instead of happy? Was she falling under the charm of all the *stuff?* The luxurious rooms, the million-dollar views?

Or was it his charm she was falling under? She thought of the smoke and jade green of those eyes, the deep self-assuredness in his voice, the way his thumb had felt, on her lip.

Whatever remained of her contentment evaporated. She felt, instead, a certain queasiness in her stomach, similar to what she felt on a roller coaster as it creaked upward toward its free fall back to earth. Was it anxiety or excitement or some diabolical mixture of both?

She touched her locket, reminding herself where these kinds of thought led. She was not even over Brent. How could she possibly be thinking about a roller-coaster ride with another man?

"Fantasy," she reminded herself sharply. "Whatever

is going on in your thoughts with Joshua Cole is not real, even if he did touch your lip." Sadly, she suspected the same was true of her relationship with Brent.

Created largely in her own mind. Was that why Melanie had sometimes looked at her with ill-disguised sympathy, as Dannie had added yet another picture to her "possible honeymoon" file? Had everyone known, long before she had, that a good relationship was not conducted from three thousand miles away and oceans apart?

Normally she would have looked in her locket when she first woke up and allowed herself to feel a longing for what was not going to be, but today she just let it settle back in the hollow of her neck, unopened.

Jake gurgled from his crib, she sat up on her elbows and watched him pull himself to his feet, begin his joyous morning bounce.

The wonderful thing about children was they did not allow one to dwell for too long in the realm of mind, they called you out of those twisting, complicated caverns of thought. They invited you to dance with the now, to laugh, to enjoy every simple pleasure. Jake was especially good at this, gurgling at her, holding out his arms, practicing a new song.

"Ba, bab, da, da, boo, boo, doo."

She could not resist. It was the first morning in a long time that she did not feel like crying. Maybe she'd start opening that locket less often! In fact, Dannie threw back the covers, went and hefted Jake from his crib, danced around the room to his music. Her bedroom door burst open and in flew Susie in her Princess Tasonja pajamas, the new bear tucked under her arm. She made for the bed and began jumping.

Normally Dannie would not encourage jumping on

the bed, but the children were on holidays. For another few hours, anyway. This might be as good as it got.

She threw her own caution to the wind, and baby in arms, jumped on the bed with Susie. They jumped and then all fell down in a heap of helpless giggles.

The room grew very quiet. She realized they were no longer alone. Dannie, upside down in the bed, tilted her head just a little bit.

Joshua Cole stood in the doorway, a faint smile tickling his lips. Unlike them, he was not in pajamas, though dressed more casually than he had been yesterday, in crisp khaki hiking pants, a pressed shirt. He had obviously showered and shaved, his golden-brown hair was darkened by the damp, his face had that smooth look of a recent close encounter with a razor that made Dannie want to touch it, to see if it felt as soft as it looked.

He took a sip of steaming coffee, drawing her eyes to his lips. She wondered how he'd feel if she waltzed over and put her thumb on his lips!

She wondered how *she'd* feel.

Like an idiot, probably. World's Sexiest Bachelor could pull off such nonsense with panache. World's Frumpiest Nanny, not so much.

Naturally, he had caught her at her frumpy best.

Her pajamas were baggy red flannel trousers with a drawstring waistline. She had on a too-large man's white T-shirt that fit comfortably over her extra protective padding. Too late, she remembered the shirt claimed she'd gotten lei'd in Hawaii.

His eyes lingered there for a touch too long. "Have you been to Hawaii?" he asked.

"No, I'm afraid I haven't. This was a gift from a friend."

"Ah. You'd love it there."

How would you know what I'd love? she thought grumpily. No two worlds had probably ever been further apart than his and hers. However, if Hawaii was even a fraction as gorgeous as this apartment, he was probably right.

"The air there smells like your perfume," he said softly.

She went very still. It was a line, obviously. The lame line of a guy whose lame lines had scored him lots of points with women a lot more sophisticated than her.

"I'm not wearing perfume," she said, letting the grumpiness out.

"Really?" He looked genuinely astounded, as if he'd meant it about Hawaii smelling like her.

She resisted an impulse to give her armpits a quick, subtle sniff. And then she realized that she was having this intimate conversation while lying upside down with a baby on her tummy.

She scrambled to sitting, juggling Jake. Her hair was flying all over the place, hissing with static, and she ran a self-conscious hand through it, trying to tame it.

He took another sip of his coffee. "Maybe it's your hair that made me think of Hawaii."

The flattery was making her flustered. A different woman, which she suddenly found herself wishing she was, would know how to respond to that. A different woman might giggle and blink her eyes and talk about skinny-dipping in the warm waters of the Pacific. With him.

Even *thinking* about skinny-dipping made her blush. Thinking of skinny-dipping anywhere in the vicinity of him made her feel as if she should go to confession. And she wasn't even Catholic!

Besides, she was sworn off men. And romance. And most certainly off skinny-dipping! Though it did seem like a bit of a shame to swear off something before even trying it.

Having thoroughly rattled her, he smiled with cat-that-got-the-cream satisfaction.

"I'm having some breakfast sent up," he said. "Fruit, yogurt. Any other requests?"

"I have to have Huggi Bears for breakfast," Susie told him.

"She doesn't," Dannie said firmly. "Yogurt is just fine. If you'll excuse us for a minute, I'll make myself presentable. And the children. Of course."

"I thought you were quite presentable. Don't feel you have to dress for breakfast. I want you to feel at home here."

"Why? We're leaving."

"Until you do," he said smoothly, and then shut the door quietly and left them alone.

A few minutes later she had the children washed and dressed. Dannie actually found herself lamenting the lack of choice in the clothing she had brought, but wore the nicest things she had packed, a pinstripe navy blue blazer and matching slacks. Like most of her clothes, the slacks were protesting her weight gain and were just a touch too snug. Thankfully the blazer covered the worst of it! The outfit was decidedly businesslike, almost in defiance of his invitation to make themselves at home. At the last moment she added a hint of makeup, ridiculously grateful there was some in her bag left over from her last trip.

He was being particularly charming this morning. That would come naturally to him. She needn't be flattered by it. Or worse, wonder what he wanted. She had nothing a man like that would want, even with the addition of mascara!

When she came out, the breakfast bar had been set up with platters of fresh fruit and croissants. Several child-size boxes of cereal, including Huggi Bears were available. There were choices of milk, chocolate milk or juice, the coffee smelled absolutely heavenly.

What would it be like to live like this? To just snap your fingers and have a feast including Huggi Bears delivered instantly?

It would make a person spoiled rotten, she thought. Emphasis on the *rotten*.

Or make them feel as if they had died and gone to heaven, she thought as she took a sip of the coffee. It was even richer and more satisfying than it had smelled.

It renewed her commitment to taking the children home. Before she was spoiled for real life. Before she started wanting and expecting luxuries she was never going to have.

"Let's take it out on the terrace," he suggested. He took the baby from her with more ease than she would have expected after just one day. When she joined him outside, he was spooning yogurt into Jake who was cooperatively opening his mouth like a baby bird waiting for a worm.

Susie had chosen one of the tiny boxes of Huggi Bears. It was the annoying kind that claimed it could be used as a bowl, but never quite worked properly. Still, Susie insisted she had to have it out of the box, and by the time Dannie had it opened along all the dotted lines and had poured the milk, she was cursing Joshua's charm and good looks, which made her feel as clumsy as if she were trying to open the box with elephants' feet instead of hands!

She made herself focus on the view, which was spectacular in the early morning light. The sea breeze was fresh and scented. She wondered what Hawaii smelled like.

She ordered herself just to enjoy this place and this moment, but it proved to be impossible. She needed to know what happened next. It was just her nature.

"So, may I ask what arrangements you've made for the children and me?" The thought of traveling again so soon exhausted her. The thought of staying here with him was terrifying.

It gave new meaning to being caught between a rock and a hard place.

"Well," he said, and smiled widely, "I have a surprise for you."

Danielle was one of those people who did not care much for surprises. It was part of being the kind of person who liked to know what was going to happen next.

"I'm flying out to look at a property for a few days. It's called the Moose Lake Lodge. Susie mentioned camping, so I thought she'd love it. All of us. A vacation in the British Columbia wilderness."

"We're going camping?" Susie breathed. "I love camping!"

"You don't know the first thing about camping," Dannie said.

"I do so!"

She was staring at Joshua with a growing feeling of anger. So this was why he'd been so charming this morning! Smelled like Hawaii, indeed. Her hair made him think of Hawaii. Sure it did!

"Are you telling me or consulting me?" she asked dangerously.

He pondered that for a moment. "I'd really like for you to come."

It was an evasive answer. It meant he hadn't booked them tickets home.

"The real question is *why* would you want to drag two children and a nanny along on a business trip?"

"It's not strictly business."

She raised an eyebrow and waited.

"You know as well as I do Melanie will kill me if I send the kids home after I promised her I'd give them a holiday."

It still wasn't the whole truth. She could feel it.

"Say yes," Susie said, slipping her hand into Dannie's and blinking at her with her most adorable expression. "Please say yes. Camping."

Everything in her screamed no.

Except for the part of her that screamed yes.

The part of her that *begged* her to, just once, say yes to the unexpected. Just once to not know what the day held. To not have a clue. To just once embrace a surprise instead of rejecting it.

To leave the safe haven of her predictable, controlled world.

What had her controlled world given her so far? Despite her best efforts, she had ended up with her heart broken, anyway.

"What do you mean, *you're* flying?" she asked, looking for a way to ease into accepting, not wanting to say an out-and-out yes as if the promise of an adventure was more than poor, boring her could refuse.

Not wanting to appear like a staid nanny who'd been offered a rare chance to be spontaneous.

"I have a pilot's license," he said. "I fly my own plane."

There was that feeling in her stomach again, of a roller coaster chugging up the steep incline. "Is that safe?" she demanded.

"More safe than getting in your car every day," he said. "Did you know that you have more chance of dying in your own bathroom than you do of dying on an airplane?"

Who could argue with something like that? Who could ever look at their own bathroom in the same way after hearing something like that?

That was the problem with a man like Joshua Cole. He could turn everything around: make what had always seemed safe appear to be the most dangerous thing of all.

For wasn't the most dangerous thing of all to have died without ever having lived? Wasn't the most dangerous thing to move through life as if on automatic pilot, not challenged, not thrilled, not engaged?

Engaged. She hated that word with its multitude of meanings. She thought she had been engaged. For the first time she did not touch her locket when she thought about it.

She took a deep breath, squeezed Susie's hand. "All right," she said. "When would you like us to be ready?"

Dannie had never flown in a small plane before. Up until getting on the plane, her stomach had been in knots about it. But watching Joshua conduct extremely precise preflight checks on the aircraft calmed her. The man radiated confidence, ease, certainty of his own abilities.

The feeling of calm increased as she settled the children, Jake in his car seat, and then she took the passenger seat right beside Joshua.

She loved the look on his face as he got ready to fly, intensely focused and relaxed at the very same time. He had the air of a man a person could trust with their life, which of course was exactly what she was doing.

The level of trust surprised her. At this time yesterday, getting off an airplane after having read about him,
she had been prepared to dislike him. When he hadn't
arrived at the airport, she had upgraded to intense dislike.

But after seeing him in his own environment, and
now in charge of this plane, she realized the mix-up at
the airport probably had been Melanie's. Joshua gave
the impression of a man who took everything he did
seriously and did everything he did well.

Still, to go from being prepared to dislike someone
to feeling this kind of trust in less than twenty-four
hours might not be a good thing. She might be falling
under his legendary, lethal charm, just like everyone
else.

Of course she was! Why else had she agreed to fly off
into the unknown with a man who was, well, unknown?

She did touch her locket then, a reminder that even
the known could become unknown, even the predictable
could fail.

Before she really had time to prepare herself, the
plane was rumbling along the airstrip and then it was
lifting, leaving the bonds of gravity, taking flight.

Dannie was surprised, and pleasantly so, to discover
she liked small airplanes better than big ones. She could
watch her pilot's face, she could feel his energy, he did
not feel unknown at all. In fact, she had a sense of
knowing him deeply as she watched his confident hands
on the controls, as she studied his face.

He glanced at her, suddenly, and grinned.

For a second he was that boy she had seen in the
photo on the beach, full of mischief and delight in life.
For a second he was that football player in the other
photo, confident, sure of his ability to tackle whatever
the world threw at him.

Something had changed him since those photos were taken. She had not been aware he carried a burden until she saw it fall away as they soared into the infinite blue of the sky.

"You love this," she guessed.

"It's the best," he said, and returned his attention to what he was doing. And she turned hers to the world he had opened up for her. A world of such freedom and beauty it could hardly be imagined. Joshua pointed out landmarks to her, explained some of the simpler things he was doing.

An hour or so later he circled a lake, the water dark denim blue, lovely cabins on spacious tree-filled lots encircling it. Wharves reached out on the water. Except for the fact it was too early in the year for people to be here, it looked like a poster for a perfect summer. Still, she was actually sorry when the flight was over.

A car waited for them at the end of the runway, and introductions were made. Sally and Michael Baker were an older couple, the lines of living outdoors deeply etched in both their faces. They were unpretentious, dressed casually in jeans and lumber jackets. Dannie liked them immediately.

And she liked it that Joshua did not introduce her as a nanny, but said instead that his sister had sent her along because she didn't trust him completely with her children!

The Bakers had that forthright and friendly way about them that made children feel instantly comfortable. Jake went into Sally's arms eagerly.

"I think he's been waiting all his short life to have a grandmother," Joshua said.

"He doesn't have a grandmother?" Sally asked, appalled.

"The kids paternal grandparents are in Australia. My mom and dad were killed in an accident when I was growing up."

Melanie had told Dannie her parents were gone, but never the circumstances. Dannie had assumed they were older, and that they had died of natural causes. Now she wondered if that was the burden he carried, and she also noted how quickly he had revealed that to the Bakers.

There was a great deal to know about this man. But to know it was to invite trouble. Because even knowing that he'd lost his parents when he was young caused a growing softness toward him.

"That must have been very hard," Sally clucked, her brown eyes so genuinely full of concern.

"Probably harder on my sister than me," he said. "She was older."

Suddenly Dannie saw Melanie's attitude toward her brother, as if he was a kid, instead of a very successful man, in a totally different light.

Michael packed their things in the back of an SUV, and they drove toward the lake. Soon they were on a beautiful road that wound around the water, trees on one side, the lake, sparkling with light, on the other.

Then they came into a clearing. A beautiful, ancient log lodge was facing the lake at one end of it, gorgeous lawns and flower beds sweeping down to the sandy shores. Scattered in on the hill behind it were tiny log cabins of about the same vintage.

"It's beautiful," Dannie breathed. More than beautiful. Somehow this place captured a feeling: summer laughter, campfires, water games, children playing tag in the twilight.

A children's playground was on part of the huge

expanse of lawn before the beach, and Susie began squirming as soon as she saw it.

"Is that a tree fort?" she demanded. "I want to play!"

Sally laughed. "Of course you want to play. You've been cooped up in a plane. Why don't I watch the kids at the park, while Michael helps you two get settled?"

Dannie expected some kind of protest from Susie, but there was none. As soon as the car door opened, she bolted for the playground.

Michael and Joshua unloaded their bags, and they followed Michael up a lovely wooden boardwalk that started behind the main lodge, wound through whispering aspens, spruce and fur. The smell alone, sweet, pure, tangy, nearly took Dannie's breath away. The boardwalk came to a series of stone stairs set in the side of the hill, and at the top of that was the first of about a dozen cabins that looked through the trees to the glittering surface of the lake.

The cabin had a name burned on a wooden plaque that hung above the stairs to the porch.

Angel's Rest.

There were a pair of rocking chairs on the covered, screened-in front porch. The logs and flooring were gray with age, the chinking and the trim around the paned window was painted white. A window box was sadly empty. Dannie could imagine bright red geraniums blooming there. A worn carpet in front of a screen door said Welcome.

Michael opened the door, which squeaked outrageously and somehow only added to the rustic charm. He set their bags inside.

It occurred to her she and Joshua were staying together, under the same roof. Why was it different from how staying under the same roof had been last night?

The cabin was smaller, for one thing, everything about it more intimate than the posh interior of Joshua's apartment. This was a space that was real. The decades of laughter, of family, soaked right into the cozy atmosphere.

"This is our biggest cabin," Michael said. "There's two bedrooms down and the loft up. Sometimes the kids sleep on the porch on hot nights, though it's not quite warm enough for that, yet."

"How wonderful there's a place left in the world where it's safe enough for the kids to sleep out on an unlocked porch," Dannie said.

Michael nodded. "My daughter and her kids usually take it for the whole summer, but—" He stopped abruptly and cleared his throat. "Dinner is at the main lodge. See you there around six. There's always snacks available in the kitchen if you need something before then."

And then he closed the door and left them.

Alone.

The cabin was more than quaint, it was as if it was a painting entitled *Home*. There were colorful Finnish rag rugs over plank flooring. An old couch, with large faded cabbage roses on the upholstery, dominated the living room decor. Inside, where the logs had not been exposed to the weather, they were golden, glowing with age and warmth. A river rock fireplace, the face blackened from use, had two rocking chairs painted bright sunshine yellow, in front of it.

Maybe it was that feeling of home that made her venture into very personal territory. Standing in this place, with him, made her feel connected to him, as if all the warmth and love of the families who had gathered in this place had infused it with a spirit of caring.

"I can't believe I've worked for Melanie for months

and didn't know about your parents. I knew they had passed, but I didn't know the circumstances."

"It was a car accident. She doesn't talk about it."

"Do you?"

He shrugged. "We aren't really talkers in our family."

"Doers," she guessed.

"You got it." Without apology, almost with warning. No sympathy allowed. Don't go there. To prove the point, he began exploring the cabin, and she could tell his assessment of the place was somewhat clinical, as if he was deliberately closing himself off to the whispers of its charm.

He was studying the window casings, which were showing slight signs of rot, scowling at the floors that looked decidedly splintery. He went up the stairs to the loft.

"I'll take this room," he called.

She knew she shouldn't go up there, but she did. She went and stood behind him. The loft room was massive. The stone chimney from downstairs continued up the far wall, and there was another fireplace. A huge four-poster bed, antique, with a hand-crafted quilt took up the greater part of the space.

He was looking under the bed.

"Boogeymen?" she asked.

He hit his head pulling out from under the bed, surprised that she was up here. "Mice."

The shabby romance of the place was obviously lost on him. "And?"

"Mouse free. Or cleaned recently."

She was afraid of mice. He was afraid of caring. Maybe it was time for at least one of them to confront their fears.

"Joshua, I'm sorry about your parents. That must

have been incredibly hard on you." She said it even though he had let her know it was off-limits.

He went over and opened a closet door, peered in. She had a feeling he was already making architectural drawings, plans, notes.

"Thanks," he said. "It was a long time ago."

"What are your plans for this place?" she said, trying to respect his obvious desire not to go there. "If you acquire it?"

"I want to turn it into a Sun resort. So that means completely revamping the interiors of these cabins, if we kept them at all. Think posh hunting lodge, deep, distressed leather furniture, a bar, good art, bearskin rugs."

She actually felt a sense of loss when he said that.

"For activities," he continued, "overnight camping trips, rock climbing, hiking, a row of jet skis tied to a new wharf."

She winced at that.

"Five-star dining in the main lodge, a lounge, some of the cabins with their own hot tubs."

"Adult only?" She felt her heart sinking. How could he be so indifferent to what this place was meant to be?

"That's what we do."

"What a shame. This place is crying for families. It feels so empty without them."

"Well, that's not what Sun does."

"Is it because of your own family?" she asked softly, having to say it, even if it did cross the boundaries in his eyes. "Is that why you cater to people who don't have families around them? Because it's too painful for you to go there?"

He stopped, came out of the closet, looked at her with deep irritation. "I don't need to be psychoanalyzed. You sound like my sister."

She had hit a nerve. She saw that. And she saw that he was right. Staying at his place, seeing him with the children, riding in his airplane, being alone in this cabin with him had all created a false sense of intimacy.

She was the nanny, the employee. She had no right to probe into his personal life. She had no right to think of him on a personal level.

But she already was! How did you backpedal from that?

"I'm sorry, Mr. Cole," she said stiffly.

The remote look left his face immediately. He crossed the room to her, she was aware how much taller he was when he looked down at her.

"Hey, I didn't mean to hurt your feelings."

"You didn't."

"Yes, I did. I can see it in your face."

"I'm sure you're imagining things."

"No, I'm not."

"Now you're being too personal, Mr. Cole."

He stared at her. "Are we having a fight?"

"I think so." Though after what she'd grown up with, this wouldn't even qualify as a squabble.

He started to laugh, and then surprisingly so did she, and the sudden tension between them dissipated, only to be replaced with a different kind of tension. Hot and aware. She could feel his breath on her cheek.

"Please don't call me Mr. Cole again."

"All right, Joshua."

"Just for the record, I didn't start running adult only resorts because of my parents." For a moment there was a pain so great in his eyes she thought they would both drown in it.

It seemed like the most reasonable thing in the world to reach out and touch his cheek, to cup his jawline in her palm and to rest her fingertips along the hard plain of his cheekbones.

His cheek was beginning to be ever so slightly whisker roughened. His skin felt unexpectedly sensual, cool and taut, beneath the palm of her hand.

He leaned toward her. For a stunning moment she thought he was going to tell her something. Something important. Maybe even the most important thing about him.

And then, the veil came down in his eyes, and something dangerous stirred in that jade surface. He was going to kiss her. She knew she should pull away, but she was helpless to do so. And then he reeled back as if he had received an electric shock, looked embarrassed, turned back to his inspection of the cabin.

She was way too aware of that big bed in this room, of the fireplace, of the pure and rugged romance of it.

"Uncle! Dannie!" Susie burst through the door downstairs. "Isn't this place the best? The best ever? You have to come see the tree fort. Sally said maybe I could sleep in it. Do you want to sleep in it with me?"

Now, that would be so much better than sleeping in here, with him. Even though she would be in a different room, this loft space was so open to the rest of the cabin below it. She would be able to imagine him here even as she slept in another room. She might even be pulled here, in the darkest night, when the heart spoke instead of the head.

Her eyes went once more to the bed. She was aware that Joshua had stopped and was watching her.

"Where are you?" Susie called.

"Up here. But coming down." Away from temptation.

Dannie ran down the steps, relieved by the distraction of the children.

Her job, she reminded herself sternly, her priority.

"Do you want to pick a bedroom?' she asked Susie.

"No, I want to *camp* in the tree fort. It's the best," Susie said, hugging herself and turning in delirious circles. "Moose Lake Lodge is the best!"

"The best," Dannie agreed halfheartedly, knowing the future of Moose Lake Lodge rested with someone who had quite a different vision of what *best* was.

But why did she feel that underneath that exterior of a cool, professional, hard-hearted businessman, Joshua was something quite different?

"I have to change," Dannie said, suddenly aware her suit was hopelessly wrong for this place. Luckily, in anticipation of a holiday, she had packed some casual slacks and T's. "Pick a room," she told Susie, "just in case you don't like camping in the tree fort."

Susie rolled her eyes at that impossibility but picked out a room. Then Dannie grabbed her suitcase and ducked into the other one.

Her mind went to that encounter with Joshua in the loft. If that kiss had been completed would she know who Joshua *really* was? Or would she be more confused than ever?

She saw herself in the old, faintly warped mirror. The first thing she noticed was not the extra ten or fifteen pounds of sadness that she carried, but the locket winking at her neck.

She touched it, then on impulse took it off and tucked it into the pocket of her suitcase. She told herself the gesture had no meaning. The locket was just too delicate for this kind of excursion.

Unwelcome, the thought blasted through her mind that she was also way too delicate for this—still fragile, still hurting.

And despite that, she would have kissed him if he had not pulled away! She put on a fresh pair of yoga pants and a matching T-shirt, regarded her reflection and was a little surprised to feel voluptuous rather than fat.

That assessment should have convinced her to put the locket back on, a constant reminder of the pain of engaging.

But she didn't. She left it right where it was.

CHAPTER FIVE

THE thing Joshua Cole loved about flying was that it was a world accessed only through absolute control, through a precision of thought and through self-discipline that only other pilots fully understood. Flying gave a sense of absolute freedom, but only after the strictest set of rules had been adhered to.

Business was much the same way. Hard work, discipline, precision of thought, all led to a predictable end result, a tremendous feeling of satisfaction, of accomplishment.

But relationships—that was a different territory altogether. They never seemed to unfold with anything like predictability. There was no hard-and-fast set of rules to follow to keep you out of trouble. No matter what you did, the safety net was simply not there.

Take the nanny, for instance. Not that he was having a relationship with her. But a man could become as enraptured by the blue of her eyes as he was held captive by the call of the sky.

He had seen something in her when they flew that he had glimpsed, too, when she had come out of her bedroom at his apartment, with Jake wrapped in that pure white towel, her blouse sticking to her, the laughter still shining in her eyes. Dannie Springer had a rare ability to experience wonder, to lose herself in the moment.

Something about her contradictions, stern and playful, pragmatic and sensitive, made him feel vulnerable. And off course. And it seemed the harder he tried to exert his control over the situation the more off course he became.

For instance, when he could feel her probing the tragedy of his parents' deaths, he had done what he always did: erected the wall.

But the fact that he had hurt her, while trying to protect himself, had knocked that wall back down as if it was constructed of paper and Popsicle sticks, not brick and mortar and steel, not any of the impenetrable materials he had always assumed it was constructed of.

In the blink of an eye, in as long as it took to draw a breath, he had gone from trying to push her away to very nearly telling her his deepest truth. He'd almost told her about his son. He had never told anyone about that. Not even his sister. To nearly confide in a woman who was virtually a stranger, despite the light of wonder that had turned her eyes to turquoise jewels while they flew, was humbling. He prided himself on control.

And it had gone from bad to worse, from humbling to humiliating. Because that flash moment of vulnerability had made him desperate to change the subject.

And he had almost done so. With his lips.

And though he had backed away at exactly the right moment, what he felt wasn't self-congratulatory smugness at his great discipline. No, he felt regret.

That he hadn't tasted the fullness of those lips, even if his motives had been all wrong.

"Just to get it over with," he muttered out loud.

He heard her come back into the main room below him and was drawn to the railing that overlooked it.

She had changed into flared, stretchy pants that rode low on the womanly curves of her hips. She was wearing sandals that showed off those adorable toes.

Just to get it over with? Who was he kidding? He suspected a person never got over a woman like Dannie, especially if he made the mistake of tasting her, touching his lips to the cool fullness of hers. If he ever got tired of her lips—fat chance—there would be her delectable little toes to explore. And her ears. And her hair, and her eyes.

Just like a baby, wrapped in a blue blanket, those eyes of hers, turquoise and haunting, would find their way into his mind for a long, long time after she was the merest of memories.

Only, though, if he took it to the next level. Which *he* wasn't going to. No more leaning toward her, no more even thinking of sharing his deepest secrets with her.

He barely knew her.

She was his niece and nephew's nanny. Getting to know her on a different level wouldn't even be appropriate. There were things that were extremely attractive about her. So what? He'd been around a lot of very attractive women. And he'd successfully avoided entanglement with them all.

Of course, with all those others he had the whole bag of tricks that money could buy to give the illusion of involvement, without ever really investing anything. It had been a happy arrangement in every case, the women delighted with his superficial offerings, he delighted with the emotional distance he maintained.

Dannie Springer would ask more of him, expect more, deserve more. Which was why it was such a good thing he had pulled back from the temptation of her lips at exactly the right moment!

He hauled his bag up to the loft, changed into more-casual clothes and then went back down the stairs and outside without bothering to unpack. He paused for a moment on the porch, drinking it in.

The quiet, the forest smells, the lap of waves on the beach stilled his thoughts. There was an island in the lake, heavily timbered, a tiny cabin visible on the shore. It was a million-dollar view.

Which was about what it was going to take—a million dollars—take or give a few hundred thousand, to bring Moose Lake Lodge up to the Sun standard.

He had seen in Dannie's face that his plans appalled her. But she was clearly ruled by emotion, rather than a good sense of business.

Maybe her emotion was influencing him, because preserving these old structures would be more costly than burning them to the ground and starting again. And yet he wanted to preserve them, refurbish them, keep some of that character and solidness.

The playground would have to go, though. He could picture an outdoor bar there, lounge chairs scattered around it. A heated pool and a hot tub would lengthen the seasons that the resort could be used. A helicopter landing pad would be good, too.

And then the squeal of Susie, floating up from the playground he wanted to destroy, was followed by the laughter of Dannie. He looked toward the playground. He could clearly see the nanny was immersing herself in the moment again, chasing Susie up the ladder into the tree fort, those long legs strong and nimble. Susie burst out the other side of the fort and slid back to the ground, Dannie didn't even hesitate, sliding behind his niece.

If he knew women with more to offer than her, he suddenly couldn't think of one. He could not think of one woman he knew who would be so comfortable, so happy, flying down a children's slide!

A little distance away from Dannie and Susie, Sally was sitting on a bench with Jake at her feet. He had a little shovel in his hand, and was engrossed in filling a pail with fine sand.

Joshua wondered how he was going to tear the playground down now. Without feeling the pang of this memory. That was the problem with emotion. He should have stuck to business. He should never have brought the children here. Of course, without the children he doubted he would have been invited here himself.

For a moment, watching the activity at the playground, Joshua felt acutely the loss of his parents and the kind of moment they would never share with him. He felt his vision blurring as he looked at the scene, listened to the shouts of laughter.

He missed them, maybe more than he had allowed himself to miss them since they had died. He remembered moments like the one below him: days at the beach in particular, endless days of carefree laughter and sunshine, sand and water.

He had a moment of clarity that felt like a punch to his solar plexus.

I wanted to keep my son so I could feel that way again. A sense of family. Of belonging. Of love.

The thought had lived somewhere deep within him, waiting for this exact moment of vulnerability to burst into his consciousness. When he had given up his son, he had given up that dream. Put it behind him. Shut the door on it. Tried to fill that empty place with other things.

And not until this very moment was he aware of how badly he had failed. He snorted with self-derision.

He was one of the world's most successful men. How could he see himself as a failure?

His sister knew what he really was.

And so did he. A man who had lost something of himself.

He shook off the unwanted moment of introspection. Though he had planned to move away from the group at the playground and go in search of Michael to begin to discuss business, he found himself moving toward them instead.

With something to prove.

Just like kissing Dannie might get it out of his system, might prove the fantasy was much more delightful than the reality could ever be, so was that scene down there.

That happy little scene was just begging to be seen with the filters removed: the baby stinking, Susie cranky and demanding.

Sally looked up and smiled at him as he crossed the lawn toward them. "Glad you arrived," she said. "I was just going to see about dinner."

And then she got up and strolled away, leaving him with Jake. After a moment considering his options, Joshua sat down on the ground beside his nephew. Just as he'd suspected: reality was cold and gritty, not comfortable at all.

And then he looked through a plastic tub of toys, found another shovel and helped Jake fill a bucket.

Just as he'd suspected: boring.

And then he tipped the bucket over and saw the beginning of a sand castle. Jake took his little shovel and smashed it, chortling with glee.

Susie arrived, breathless. "Are you making something?"

Dannie's long length of leg moved into his range of vision. She was hanging back just a bit. Sensing, just as he did, that something dangerous was brewing here.

He looked up at her. He didn't know why he noticed, but the locket was missing. Just in case he hadn't already figured out something dangerous was brewing here.

He handed her a bucket, as if he was project manager on a huge construction site. *Thatta boy,* he congratulated himself. *Take charge.* "Do you and Susie want to haul up some water from the lake? We'll make a sand castle."

Before he knew it, he wasn't bored, but he was still plenty uncomfortable. Take charge? Working this closely with Dannie, he was finding it hard to even take a breath, he was so aware of her! She kept casting quick glances at him, too. It was so junior high! Building a Popsicle bridge for the science fair with the girl you had a secret crush on!

Not that he had a secret crush on her!

The castle was taking shape, multiturreted, Dannie carefully carving windows in the wet sand, shaping the walls of the turrets.

She had the cutest way of catching her tongue between her teeth as she concentrated. Her hair kept falling forward, and she kept shoving it impatiently back. It made him wonder what his fingers would feel like in her hair, a thought he quickly dismissed in favor of helping Susie build the moat and defending the castle from Jake's happy efforts to smash it with his shovel.

Before he knew it, his discomfort had disappeared, and happiness, that sneakiest of human emotions, had slipped around them, obscuring all else. It was as if fog, turned golden by morning sun, had wrapped them in a world of their own. Before he knew it, he was laughing.

And Dannie was laughing with him, and then Susie was in his arms with her thumb in her mouth, all wet and dirty and sandy, and the baby smelled bad, and reality was strangely and wonderfully better than any fantasy he had ever harbored.

Something in him let go, he put business on the back burner. For some reason, though he was undeserving of it, he had been given this gift. A few days to spend with his niece and nephew in one of the most beautiful places he had ever seen or been.

A few days to spend with a woman who intrigued him.

By the next day, he and Dannie settled into a routine that felt decidedly domestic. It should have felt awkward playing that role with her, but it didn't. It felt just like walking into the cottage Angel's Rest had felt, like coming home.

Sally prepared the most wonderful food he had ever eaten: old-fashioned food, stew and buns for supper the evening before, biscuits and jam for breakfast, thick sandwiches on homemade bread for lunch.

The lodge, magnificently constructed, always smelled of bread rising and baking and of fresh-brewed coffee. In the chill of the evening last night, there had been a fire going, children's board games and toys spread out on the floor in front of it.

The second day unfolded in endless spring sunshine. They played in the sand, they went on a nature walk, he rowed the kids around in the rowboat. When the kids settled in for their afternoon naps, he and Dannie sat on the front porch of Angel's Rest.

"Kids are exhausting," he told her, settling back in his chair, glad to be still, looking at the view of the little cabin on the island. "I need a nap more than them."

"You are doing a great job of being an uncle. World's Best Builder of Sand Castles."

Somehow that meant more to him than being bestowed with the title of World's Sexiest Bachelor.

"Thanks. You're doing a great job of…being yourself." That made her blush. He liked it. He decided to make her blush more. "World's Best Set of Toes."

"You're being silly," she said, and tried to hide her naked toes behind her shapely calves.

Today she was wearing sawed-off pants he thought were called capris. They hugged her delicious curves in the most delightful way.

"I know. Imagine that. Come on. Be a sport. Give me a peek of those toes."

She hesitated, took her foot out from behind her leg, and wiggled her toes at him.

He laughed at her daring, and then so did she. He thought it would be easy to make it a mission to make her laugh…and blush.

"I love the view from here," Dannie told him, hugging herself, tucking her toes back under her chair. "Especially that cabin. If I ever had a honeymoon, that's where." She broke off, blushing wildly.

If there was one thing a guy as devoted to being single as he was did not ever discuss it was weddings. Or honeymoons. But his love of seeing her blush got the better of him.

"What do you mean if?" he teased her. "If ever toes were made to fit a glass slipper, it's those ones. Some guy is going to fall for your feet, and at your feet, and marry you. You'll spend your whole honeymoon getting chased around with him trying to get a nibble of them. I'm surprised it hasn't happened already."

Even though the teasing worked, her cheeks staining to the color of crushed raspberries, the thought of some lucky guy chasing her around made him feel miserable.

"Oh," she said, her voice strangled, even as she tried to act casual, "I've given up Cinderella dreams. Men are mostly cads in sheep's clothing."

Her attempt at being casual missed, and then she touched her neck, where the locket used to be.

"How right you are," he said, but he felt very sorry about it, and he knew he was exactly the wrong guy to correct her misconceptions. Who had lured her and the kids here veiling another motive, after all?

Who looked at her lips and her toes and her hair and fought an increasingly hard battle not to steal a little taste, no matter what the consequences?

He knew he shouldn't ask. But he did, anyway. "Did he hurt you badly?"

"Who?" she croaked, wide-eyed.

He sighed. "The professor."

Her hand dropped away from her neck. "I'm embarrassed to be so transparent."

"Good. I hope it makes you blush again. Did he?"

She contemplated that for a moment and then said quietly, "No, I hurt myself."

But he doubted if that was completely true, and he felt a sudden murderous desire to meet the jerk that had hurt her. And another desire to see if he could chase the sudden sadness from her eyes. With his lips.

But something kept him from giving in to the little devil that sat on his shoulder, prodding him with the proverbial pitchfork and saying with increasing force and frequency, *Kiss her. No one will get hurt.*

The thought was in such contrast to the innocence of playing tag in the trees until they were breathless with laughter, in such contrast to the wholesome fun of wading and splashing along the shorelines of a lake too cold yet to swim in.

He was not looking forward to another night in the cabin with her, once the children were in bed, but the angel that sat on her shoulder must have been stronger than the devil on his.

Because after another incredible supper, fresh lake trout cooked by Sally, Dannie announced she and Susie would be sleeping in the tree fort. Ridiculously, he heard himself saying he would join them.

He had the worst sleep of his life in the tree fort, with Susie between his and Dannie's sleeping bags, the baby in a huge wicker basket at their heads, cooing happily from his nest of warm blankets.

Dannie was so close, he could touch that incredible hair, but he didn't. She was so close he could smell the Hawaiian flower scent of her. He lay awake looking at the incredible array of stars overhead, and listening to her breathing, and in the morning, he felt cold and cramped and more alive than he had felt in a long, long time.

He woke up looking into Dannie's sleep-dazed turquoise eyes, and wondered how on earth he was ever going to go back to life as he had known it.

The carefree stay here at Moose Lake Lodge was about as far from his high-powered life as he could have gotten. He didn't check his Blackberry, there was no TV to watch. No Internet.

He had a new reality and so much of it was about Dannie: her eyes and her lips and the way she tossed her hair. How she looked with her slacks rolled up and smudged with dirt, hugging the womanliness of her curves, her bare toes curling in warm sand.

He saw the way she was with those kids: patient, loving, genuine. He came to look forward to her intelligence, the playful sting of exchanged insults.

He was acutely aware Dannie was the kind of woman that men, superficial creatures that they were, overlooked. But if a man was looking for a life partner—which he thankfully was not—could he do any better than her?

That morning, after the exquisite pleasure of a hot shower after a cold night, over pancakes and syrup, Sally told them she and Michael would mind the kids for the day.

"The only one who hasn't had any kind of a holiday, a break from responsibility, is Dannie. This is your last full day here. Go have some fun, you two."

His niece had been so right about him, Joshua thought. He was just plain dumb.

He turned to Dannie, humbled by Sally's consideration of her. This morning Dannie was wearing a red sweatshirt that hid some of the features that made his mouth go dry, but the jeans made up for it.

The dark denim hugged her. It occurred to him that skinny butts were highly overrated. It occurred to him that was a naughty thought for a man who was going to try his hand at being considerate.

"The whole time I've been thinking how enjoyable this experience is," Joshua admitted, "you've been doing your job, minding children."

"Oh, no," Dannie protested, "I don't feel like that at all. I once heard if you do a job you love, you'll never work a day in your life, and that's how I feel about being with Susie and Jake."

Again, Joshua was taken with what a prize she was going to make for someone. And again he was taken aback by his own reaction to that thought. Misery.

Before someone else snapped her up, could he put his own priorities on hold long enough to show her a good time? Could he trust himself, not forever, but for one day? To put her needs ahead of his own? To be considerate, instead of a self-centered jerk?

"Sally's right," he decided firmly. "It's time for your holiday."

Dannie was looking wildly uncomfortable, as if she didn't really want to spend time with him without the buffer zone of two lively and demanding children.

Which was only sensible. He was tired of her sensible side. He was annoyed at being bucked when he'd made the decision to be a better man, to be considerate and a gentleman.

"I have had a holiday, really," she insisted. "How can I eat food like Sally's, and stay in a place as beautiful as Angel's Rest and not feel as if I've had a holiday? I loved it better than a stay at a five-star resort. No offense to five-star resort owners in the vicinity."

"No," Sally said, firmly. "Today it's your turn. You have some grown-up time. Why don't you and Josh take a canoe over to the island? I'll pack you a picnic. Josh should look at it anyway, since it's part of the Moose Lake Lodge property. Many a honeymoon has taken place at that cabin!"

Despite Dannie claiming to be cynical about relationships, he did not miss the wistful look in her eyes when she heard that she had been so right about the island being an idyllic setting for a honeymoon! Joshua, good intentions aside, wasn't sure he was up to grown-up time with Dannie on an island where people had their honeymoons!

Still, he didn't miss the fact that Sally and Michael, though no business had been discussed, must be opening just a little bit to the idea of him acquiring the Lodge for Sun since they were encouraging him to see all that comprised it.

In search of perfect adventures for the clients of Sun, and in keeping with his fast-paced single lifestyle, Joshua had tried many activities, including some that might be considered hair-raising like bungee jumping and parasailing.

None of those activities had ever really fazed him, but an hour later, out in the canoe with Michael, brushing up on his canoeing skills, Joshua felt the weight of responsibility. He had canoed before, but never in waters that could kill you with cold if you capsized and had to stay in them for any length of time.

Michael assured him the island was only a twenty-minute paddle across quiet waters.

"I'll keep an eye on you," he promised. "If something goes wrong, I'll rescue you in the powerboat."

Joshua was not sure he could imagine anything that would be more humiliating than that, especially with Dannie sharing the boat with him. He was also aware Dannie's presence, besides making him aware of not wanting a rescue, made him feel responsible for another human being, something that was also new in his free-wheeling bachelor existence.

In a way it was ironic, because he shouldered tremendous responsibility. The business decisions he made literally affected the lives and livelihoods of hundreds of people.

That kind of responsibility didn't even seem real compared to having a life in his hands. Naturally he'd had his own life in his hands many times before, but if he got himself in trouble, he was the only one who suffered the consequences. Maybe the truth was he didn't really even care.

Strangely, both feelings—of not wanting to make a fool of himself in front of her and of feeling responsible for her safety—made him feel not weakened, but strengthened. Like he was manning up, assuming the ancient role of the protector, the warrior. He would never have guessed that role could feel so satisfying.

Trust Dannie not to let him relish the role for too long! He got her settled in the front of the boat—the non-control position in a canoe—and gave her a paddle for decorative purposes. He issued dire warnings about the tipiness of the contraption they were setting out in, and then he settled into his own position of navigator, course setter, and head paddler.

He was so intent on his duties, he noticed only peripherally that her red sweatshirt matched the red of the canoe, and that her rear in those jeans was something worth manning up for!

But before they were even out of the protected bay that sheltered the lodge, she turned to him in annoyance. Her cheeks were flushed with exertion, which she was bringing on herself by trying to pull the boat single-handedly through the water with her paddle!

"Look, I think this is a team activity. I'm not really the kind of girl who wants to sit in the front of the boat and look pretty, but I think we're paddling out of sync."

In other words she wasn't the kind of girl he'd gotten accustomed to.

In other words, maybe he'd been going it alone a little too much. He wasn't even sure he could play on a team anymore.

But to his surprise, as soon as he relaxed control, as

soon as he began to work with her instead of trying to do it all himself, the canoe began to cut through the water with silent speed and grace, an arrow headed straight for that island.

"That's better," she said, looking over her shoulder and grinning at him.

He wasn't quite sure when she had transformed, but somewhere in the last few days she had gone from plain to beautiful. The sun had kissed pale skin to golden, she had given up all effort to tame her luscious hair, and it curled wildly around her face, her expression seemed to become more relaxed each second that they left the children behind them.

"You are pretty," he stammered, and was amazed how he sounded. He, who had escorted some of the world's most beautiful and accomplished women, sounded like a schoolboy on his first date.

In answer, she scraped her paddle across the surface of the water, and deliberately splashed him with the icy cold lake water.

Now he could see the gypsy he had glimpsed in her before, dancing to life, especially when she laughed at his chagrin. Dannie said, with patent insincerity, "Oops."

Now, in this moment, he could see the truth of who she was, shining around her. This is what he had glimpsed when he had touched her lip with this thumb, a very long time ago, it seemed. This is what he had known about her that she had not known about herself. That she was made to dance with life, to shine with laughter, to blossom.

And in that he recognized another truth.

It was not her who was becoming transformed. It was him.

"Don't rock the boat," he said grumpily. And somehow it sounded like a metaphor for his life. Joshua Cole, entrepreneur who performed feats of daring and innovation in business, and who embraced adventure in the scant amount of time he allowed for play, did not rock the boat in that one all-important area.

Relationships. He did not even risk real involvement. He saw women a few times, and at the first hint they wanted more he made an exit. At the first sign of true intimacy of the emotional variety he was out of there. He was willing to play the game with his wallet, but he did not take chances with his heart.

Because his heart had been battered and bruised. When his parents had died, people had told him time would heal all wounds. When he had agreed with Sarah that the best thing for that baby would be to allow him to go to a loving family who were emotionally and financially mature, who were prepared for a child in every way, he had thought time would eventually lessen the ache he felt over that decision.

Maybe he had even believed that time *had* eased the pain. But he had only been kidding himself.

Outrunning something was not the same as healing. Not even close.

"Land ho," Dannie called, as they drew close to the island.

He looked at her face, shining with enthusiasm for the day, and he felt his guard slip away. He made a decision, just for today, he would engage as completely as he was able.

For her. So she could enjoy one day of being irresponsible, of having fun without the kids.

They landed the canoe, gracelessly, coming as close to tipping it as they had come yet, though thankfully the waters off the island were shallow enough that he didn't have to worry about her dying of hypothermia in them if they did capsize. Still, even with her jeans rolled up, she was wet to her knees.

He lifted the picnic basket Sally had packed for them and followed Dannie up the shoreline and left the basket there.

"I can't wait to see it," she said, and started up the path that led to the cabin. She stumbled on a root, and he reached out his hand to steady her. Somehow he never took his hand away. Hers folded into his as if it was absolutely meant to be there.

There was a well-worn path to the cabin, which was as quaint up close as it had been from far away. Like Angel's Rest, it had a name plaque hanging at the entrance to the covered, vine-twined porch.

"Love's Rhapsody," she read out loud. "Isn't that lovely?"

"Corny," he said, deciding then and there the sign was coming down the minute he owned the place

"Should we go in?" she asked. There was something about her wide-eyed wonder in the little cabin that was making him feel edgy.

"Well, yeah, it's not a church. Besides, I might own it one day. I might as well see how much money I'd have to throw at it to keep it."

She reacted as he had hoped, by glaring at him as if he had desecrated a sacred site. It was important that she know that distinction existed between them. He cynical and pragmatic, she soft and dreamy. It was important she know that that distinction existed between them, so the wall was up.

And a man needed a wall up in a place like this! He needed a wall up when he was beginning to feel all enthused about playing the protector and warrior. When he felt strangely uncertain if they should enter that sanctuary. What if whatever was in there—the spirit of romance—overcame them? What if he was helpless against it?

Annoyed with himself for so quickly breaking his vow to make the day about her instead of about him, Joshua pushed past her and shoved open the door.

His first reaction to the interior was one of relief, because the cabin was dark and musty smelling. There was absolutely nothing in it to speak of. An old antique bed, with the mattress rolled up, and the linens stored, a little table, a threadbare couch and a stone fireplace just like the one at Angel's Rest.

And yet, the fact there was so little in here, seemed to highlight that there was something in here, unseen.

"Look," she whispered, wandering over to one of the walls. "Oh, Joshua, look."

Carved lovingly into the walls, were names. Mildred and Manny, April 3, 1947, Penelope and Alfred, June 9, 1932. Sometimes it was just the couple's name, other times a heart and arrow surrounded it, sometimes a poem had been painstakingly cut out in the wall. It seemed each couple who had ever honeymooned here had left their mark on those walls.

It was hard not to be moved by the testament to love, to commitment. There really was nothing at all of material value in this cabin.

And yet there was something here so valuable it evaded being named: a history of people saying yes to the adventure of beginning a life together.

In this funny little cabin, it felt as if it was the only adventure that counted.

Cynicism would protect him from the light shining

in her eyes. But what of his vow to let her have the day she wanted?

So, when they left the cabin he took her hand again, despite the fact he wanted to shove his into his pockets, defending against what had been in there. Strangely, holding her hand seemed to still the uncertainty in him.

The island was small. They walked around the whole thing in an hour. He soon forgot his discomfort in the cabin, and found himself making it about her with amazing ease. But then, that's what being with her was like: easy and comfortable.

With just the faintest hint of sexual awareness, tingling, that added to rather than detracted from the experience of being together.

Finally they returned to the beach and opened Sally's picnic basket. She had sent them hot dogs and buns, matches and fire starter.

They gathered wood, and he lit the fire, feeling that *thing* again, the shouldering of the ancient role: *I will start the fire that will warm you.*

Obviously, the corniness from the cabin was catching!

With hot dogs blackening on sticks over an open fire, and the magic of the cabin behind him, he found himself taking a tentative step forward, wanting to be more but also to know more. Soon she would go her own way, and he would go his. It made the exchange seem risk-free.

"Tell me why you're content to raise other people's children," he said, touching the mustard at the edge of her mouth with his finger, putting that finger to his own lips, watching her eyes go as wide as if he had kissed her.

"I told you, it's a job I love. I never feel as if I'm working."

"But doesn't that make you think you are ideally suited to be a mother yourself, of your own children?"

Maybe that was too personal, because Dannie blushed wildly, as if he had asked her to be the mother of his children!

He loved that blush! Before her, when was the last time he had even met a woman who still blushed?

"It's because of the heartbreak," he guessed softly, looking at the way she was focusing on her hot dog with sudden intensity. "Will you tell me about it?"

This was exactly the kind of question he *never* asked. But suddenly he really wanted to know. He knew about things you kept inside. You thought they'd gone away, when in fact they were eating you from the inside out.

"No," she said. "You're burning your hot dog."

"That's how I like them. What was his name?"

She glared at him. Her expression said, *leave it.* But her voice said, reluctantly, "Brent."

"Just for the record, I've always hated that name. Let me guess. A college professor?"

"It's not even an interesting story."

"All stories are interesting."

"Okay. You asked for it. Here is the full pathetic truth. Brent was a college professor. I was a student. He waited until I wasn't in any of his classes to ask me out. We dated for a few months. I fell in love and thought he did, too. He had a trip planned to Europe, a year's sabbatical from teaching, and he went."

"He didn't ask you to go?"

"He asked me to wait. He made me a promise."

Joshua groaned.

"What are you making noises for?"

"If he loved you he would never, ever have gone to Europe without you."

"Thank you. Where were you when I needed you? He promised he would come back, and we'd get married. I took the nanny position temporarily."

"No ring, though," Joshua guessed cynically.

"He gave me a locket!"

"With his own picture inside? Thought pretty highly of himself, did he?" It was the locket she'd worn when he first met her. That she'd put away. What did it mean that she had taken it off?

That it was a good time for her to have this conversation? He knew himself to be a very superficial man, the wrong person to be navigating the terrifying waters of a woman's heartbreak. What moment of insanity had gripped him, encouraged her confidences? But now that she'd got started, it was like a dam bursting.

"At first he e-mailed every day, and I got a flood of postcards. It made me do really dumb things. I...I used all my savings and bought a wedding gown."

Her face was screwing up. She blinked hard. Maybe wheedling this confession out of her hadn't been such a good idea after all.

"It's like something out of a fantasy," she whispered. "Lace and silk." She was choking now. "It was all a fantasy. Such a safe way to love somebody, from a distance, anticipating the next contact, but never having to deal with reality.

"Can I tell you something truly awful? Something I don't even think I knew until just now? The longer he stayed away, the more elaborate and satisfying my fantasy love for him became."

She was crying now. No mascara, thank God. He patted her awkwardly on the shoulder, and when that didn't seem to give her any comfort, or him either, he threw caution to the wind, and his hot dog into the fire. He pulled her into his chest.

Felt her hair, finally.

It felt as he had known it would feel, like the most expensive and exquisite of silks.

It smelled of Hawaii, exotic and floral. This was why he was so undeserving of her trust: she was baring her soul, he was being intoxicated by the scent of her hair.

"Actually," she sniffed, "Brent was the final crack in my romantic illusions. My parents had a terrible relationship, constant tension that spilled over into fighting. When I met Brent, I hoped there was something else, and there was, but it turned out to be even more painful. Oh, I hope I don't sound pathetic. The I-had-a-bad-childhood kind of person."

"Did you?" he asked, against his better judgment. Of course the smell of her hair and her soft curves pressed into his body made him feel as if he had no judgment at all, wiped out by sensory overload. And yet even for that, he registered her saying she'd had a bad childhood and he ached for her. There were things even a warrior could not hope to make right.

"Terrible," she said with a defeated sigh. "Filled with fighting and uncertainty, making up that always filled us kids with such hope and never lasted. It was terrible."

"Maybe that's why you're so invested in children. Giving them the gift of happiness that you didn't have. You do have that gift, you know. So engaged with them, so genuinely interested in them."

"Did you have a good childhood?" she asked, and her wistfulness tore through the barriers around his heart that usually kept him from sharing too deeply with anyone.

"Camelot," he said. "I can't remember one bad thing.

I often wonder if every family is only allotted so much luck, and we used ours up."

"Oh, Joshua," she said softly.

"My parents were crazy about each other. And about us. We were the fun family on the block—my dad coaching the Little League team, my mom filling the rubber swimming pool for all the neighborhood kids. And it was all so genuine. I see parents sometimes who I think are following a rule book, thinking about how it all looks to other people, but my folks weren't like that. They did these things with us because they loved to do it, not because they wanted to *look* like great parents."

"And because of that they were great parents."

"The best," he remembered softly. "Every year for three weeks they rented a cottage on the seashore. We had these long days of swimming and playing in the sand, we had bonfires out front on the beach every night. There wasn't even a TV set. If it rained, we played Monopoly or Sorry or cards."

He realized he had never felt that way again. Ever. Not until he had come here.

And to feel that way was to leave yourself open to a terrible hurt.

Was he ready?

A sudden sound made him jerk up from her. Without his noticing, so engrossed in protecting her and comforting her, and sharing his own secret memories with her, the wind had come up on the lake.

Some warrior. Some protector! He had not tied the canoe properly. It had yanked free of its mooring, the sound he had heard was it crashing into a rock as it bounced away from the small island.

He ran for the water, plunged in, could not believe the cold and stopped.

"Leave it," Dannie cried.

Good advice. He should let the canoe go, but everything about Moose Lake Lodge said the Bakers were operating on a shoestring. He'd been entrusted with their canoe.

"I can't," he shouted at her, moving deeper into the water. "Can you imagine how the Bakers will react if the canoe drifts back there, empty? What about Susie?"

He took a deep breath and moved deeper into the water, felt her movement on the beach behind him.

"Stay there," he called. "I've got it under control."

He was used to speaking, and people listened. Naturally, Dannie did not. He heard her splash into the water, her shocked gasp as the icy water filled her shoes.

It made him desperate to get that canoe before they were both in deep trouble. He was up to his waist, he lunged forward, and just managed to get the rope that trailed off the bow of the boat.

He pulled it back toward shore, grabbed her elbow as he moved by, steering her in the right direction.

"I told you not to come in," he said.

"I was trying to help!" she said, unrepentant.

"Now we're both wet." But what he was thinking was it had been a long time since he had been with the kind of woman who would plunge into that water with him. He knew a lot of women who would have stood on shore, unhelpfully hysterical or more worried about her haute couture than him!

Still, they both could have got in trouble and it would have been his fault. He was aware of freezing water squeezing out of his shoes and that, wet up to his chest, his teeth were chattering wildly and in a most unmanly way.

Except for the fact it might save the Bakers some

distress, his rescue was wasted. When he inspected the canoe it had a hole the size of his fist in the bottom of it from where it had smashed into a rock.

He inspected her, too. She was wet past her waist, had her arms wrapped around herself. She was reacting to the cold in a very womanly way, and he did his best not to whistle with low appreciation.

Think, Joshua snapped at himself.

He was stranded on an island. With a beautiful woman. Who was shivering, and who had hair that smelled of Hawaii.

They were both going to have to get these wet clothes off quickly. And not in the way any red-blooded man wanted to have the first disrobing happen.

But because the May wind was like ice as the spring day lengthened and chilled, if they didn't get out of these wet clothes, there was a real chance of hypothermia.

There was only one option.

They were going to have to seek shelter in the honeymoon cabin.

Just his luck that he was going to end up half-naked in the honeymoon cabin with Dannie Springer. Maybe it was because he was shaking with cold that he couldn't quite figure out if he had landed in the middle of a dream or a nightmare.

CHAPTER SIX

DANIELLE SPRINGER had been in a few awkward situations, but this one definitely rated as Most Embarrassing, especially given the fact she was in the company of Most Sexy. If she hadn't known that about him before, she certainly couldn't miss it now that she had seen his soaked clothes mold every inch of his fine male body.

What had started off as a day full of potential, was now quickly declining toward disastrous, as quickly as darkness was sweeping over the small island.

She had broken down in front of him, shared confidences she never should have shared. When the canoe had ripped away, she'd been devastated. He had been in the middle of telling her important things, *real* things about himself. Thankfully, his own confidences had snapped her out of her self-pitying recital of woe.

Watching him push out into the water to save the canoe, she had thought sadly, only Dannie Springer would be alone on an island with a man like that, lamenting her last, lost boyfriend. It was no excuse that Joshua had encouraged her. That's what men who were successful with women did. That was their secret weapon. They listened.

Except it was becoming increasingly difficult to see Joshua in the light of his playboy reputation.

Especially after the way he had looked talking about his family, the tenderness in his voice, he seemed like the most real man she had ever met. Poor Brent seemed like a comic book character in comparison. Joshua Cole seemed genuine. That's why the *trust* element was there, despite the fact she had known him only a matter of days. That's why she had let her guard down, when she of all people, jilted, should have her guard up higher.

When had she decided it would be okay to trust him with her heart? It was the way he looked at her, compassionate intensity darkening the shade of green of his eyes. Something she interpreted as *interest,* hot, male and intoxicating was brewing just beneath the calm surface.

Yet for all that male energy—sure and strong—the way he had conducted himself over the past few days was nothing short of admirable. He was a man navigating a foreign land with the children, and yet he was doing it with grace and openness.

Even the way he plunged into the water after that canoe spoke to character. It was him, supposedly the self-centered bachelor, not her, the supposedly compassionate nanny, who had considered how others would react to the empty canoe showing up somewhere.

Dumb to plunge into the water after him, because what was she going to do? But somehow, ever since they'd gotten in that canoe together, she had felt the delicious sense of teamwork. She had plunged into the water almost on instinct. They were in this *together*.

But she was paying for her altruism now.

They were in the honeymoon cottage where hundreds of couples had shyly taken off their clothes for each other for the very first time.

And not a single one of them like this, she thought dourly. Not a single one of them because they were in imminent danger of shivering to death.

"Embarrassing," she muttered out loud.

"Forget embarrassment," he said, glancing back at her from where he was crouched in front of the fireplace, feeding little sticks into it, coaxing a bright blaze to life.

He had peeled off his sodden trousers as if it was the most natural thing in the world. Of course, for him, World's Sexiest Bachelor, it probably was.

Except for the part where he'd warned her he was doing it, giving her time to turn around.

Except for the part where he'd unearthed a container full of bedding, snapped off the lid, and tucked a blanket around himself.

He should have looked like an idiot with his flowing red tartan blanket tied in a knot at his taut stomach. Instead he looked like a chieftain, his shoulders and chest bare, his arms rippling with sinewy strength. There was a warrior cast to his face, remote and focused, as he had turned his attention to getting a fire going in the old stone fireplace.

"I can't get my jeans off," she wailed.

"What?"

"I can't get them off," she said, annoyed he was making her say it again. He had heard her the first time!

The soaked denim, which had probably been a touch snug to begin with, was stuck to her now. Her hands were so cold she couldn't make them do one thing she wanted them to do.

He turned and looked at her. "Are you asking me to help you get your pants off, Miss Pringy?"

"No!" Then with sudden rueful understanding, she said, "You like making me blush, don't you?"

"If I was considering a new hobby that would be it. I could while away hours at a time thinking up things like—"

"Now is not the time for games, Joshua! I'm just telling you I'm stuck. Just hand me a blanket."

He came across the room toward her, without the covering she had ordered, and his own blanket slipped. She held her breath, shamelessly hopeful, but he stopped and reknotted it, moved toward her.

"Just relax," he said soothingly, looking at the situation with what struck her as an annoying bent toward the analytical. She had the button undone on her jeans, and the zipper down. She had wrested the uncooperative, sodden, freezing fabric about three inches down her hips and there it was stuck, hard.

"It's because you're tense," he decided.

Taking off my pants in a room with the World's Sexiest Bachelor, and I'm tense. Go figure.

"It's because my hands are too cold." It was true her hands felt as if they had turned into icy basketballs at the ends of her wrists. But there was another problem. She was just going to have to admit it and get it over with.

"The jeans might have been a little too tight to begin with. Marginally."

"They looked fine to me," he said, apparently thinking about it. "More than fine. Great." She might have been thrilled that he'd noticed in different circumstances.

As it was, the jeans had been a bit of a challenge to get on, and that's when they'd been dry. What little devil of vanity had made her think her rear end looked good enough in them to put up with a tiny bit of discomfort?

"Look, no matter how reasonable a choice they were when they were dry, they won't come off now. They won't fit over my hips. There, am I blushing enough for you?"

His lips twitched.

"Don't laugh," she warned him.

"I won't," he said, but she could tell he was biting the inside of his cheek. Hard. He didn't speak for a minute, containing himself. "Let me help," he finally managed, and then choked. "I sound like a butler."

"Only one of us here would know what that sounded like," she warned him, but it was too late.

He was laughing, moving toward her with singleness of purpose written all over him.

"Don't touch me!" There. Self-preservation finally rising to the occasion. Where had that fine attribute of character been when she had been sobbing her heart out in his seemingly sympathetic ear?

"I can't help you without touching you."

"I don't need your help." That was a lie obvious to both of them. "You're laughing at me."

"I'm trying not to."

"Try harder."

"Okay." He crouched down, and was looking at the area where the soaked jeans were bound up around the wideness of her hips. Oddly enough, the way his eyes rested there, briefly and with heat, before returning to her face did not make her feel like a whale. At all. In fact, his laughter seemed to have died, too.

"Yes, you do," he said firmly, "need my help."

"Okay, then." She was shaking too hard to deny it any longer. She closed her eyes hard against her humiliation. "Just be quick."

"That's the first time I've ever heard that in this particular situation," he muttered.

"We are not in a *situation*," she warned him, "or not one you've ever been in before."

"You're absolutely right about that," he said.

His hands settled around the jeans. Her skin was so cold she actually felt scorched from the heat of his hands. She had to resist an impulse to wiggle into that warmth. Instead she made herself stand rigidly still. She opened her eyes just enough to squint at him undetected through the veil of her lashes.

He yanked with considerable strength, enough that she saw that lovely triceps muscle in his arm jump into gorgeous relief. Unfortunately the jeans did not budge, not a single, solitary fraction of an inch.

"Your skin feels like ice-cold marble," he noted clinically.

Somehow in her imagination, she had imagined him saying softly, *Your skin is like silk that's been heating in the sun, soft and sensual.*

When had she imagined such a thing? Practically every damn minute since she had met him, a dialogue of lust and wanting running just below her prim surface.

"Can't you relax?"

"I doubt it," she moaned, and then made the confession that made her humiliation complete. "You're going to have hurry. I think I have to go to the bathroom."

"Dannie, it would be really inadvisable for you to get us laughing right now. Really."

"Believe me, I am nowhere close to laughing." But his lips were twitching again. How had she ever thought he was handsome? He wasn't. He was like an evil leprechaun.

"Someday you'll see the humor in this," he assured her. "You'll tell your kids about it."

No, she wouldn't. Because a story like that would begin with, "Did I ever tell you how I met your dad?"

And he was not going to be the father of her children. Though suddenly she was aware she had a secret self that not only conducted entire conversations just out of range of her conscious mind, but *wished* things. Impossible things.

Green-eyed babies.

She told herself she had just gotten over another man. This was rebound lust, nothing more. But she was very aware of quite a different truth. There never had been another man, really, just a convenient fantasy, a risk-free way to play at love, a safe way to withdraw from the game while pretending to be engaged in it.

Joshua tugged again. The wet, cold, thick fabric shifted a mean half inch or so.

"Ouch. Who invented denim? What a ridiculous material," she complained.

"There's a reason they don't make swimsuits out of it," he agreed, and then broke it to her gently. "You're going to have to lie down on the bed. Hang on. I'll cut the mattress open."

He found a knife and cut the strings that were wrapped tightly around the mattress, a defense against mice.

Mice, which had probably been her greatest fear until about thirty seconds ago. Now her greatest fear was herself!

"Maybe you could just cut the jeans off," she said. She shuffled over to the bed, the jeans just down enough to impair her mobility, no dignified waltz across the cold cabin floor for her. She left great puddling footsteps in her wake.

"I'll keep that in mind as a last resort, but I might cut you by accident, so we'll try this first. Lie down."

Why didn't her fantasies *ever* work out? Every woman in the world would die to hear those words from his lips. "Don't get bossy," she said, so he'd never guess how great her disappointment was at the *way* he said that.

"Hey, if you could have followed simple instructions in the first place, you wouldn't be in this predicament."

She turned around and flopped down on the mattress, her knees hanging over. "I wasn't letting you go in that water by yourself."

"Why not?"

The truth blasted through her. *I think I'm falling in love with you. For real, damn it, not some romantic illusion I can take home and satisfy with buying dresses and planning honeymoons I know are never going to happen.*

Out loud she said, "The team thing. Okay, pull. Pull hard."

Real, she scoffed at herself. She was getting more pathetic by the day. You did not fall in love with a man in four days. Unless you were a Hollywood celebrity, which she most definitely was not.

She felt his hands, scorching hot again against the soft flesh of her hips and looked at the frown of concentration marring his handsome features.

It felt real, even if it wasn't. Of course, people who heard little voices swore that was real, too.

"Hang on," he said. He took a grip and pulled. The jeans inched down. Finally he was past the horrible hip obstacle, but now his hands rested on the top of her thighs, his thumbs brushing that delicate tissue of pure sensitivity on her inner leg. Thankfully, the skin was nearly frozen, not nearly sensitive enough to make her reach up grab his ears and order him huskily to make her warm.

He tugged again. His hands moved from the thigh

area and the jeans reluctantly parted from her frozen, pebbled skin. He yanked them free triumphantly, held them up for her to see, as if he was a hunter holding up a snake he had killed and skinned just for her.

"My skin looks like lard, doesn't it?" she demanded, watching his face for signs of revulsion. If she had seen any, she would have gotten up and marched straight back into that lake!

He was silent for a long moment. "Alabaster," he said softly.

"Huh!" Nonetheless, she was mollified for a half second or so until she thought of something else. "I hope I don't have on the panties that say Tuesday."

"Uh, no, you don't."

Suddenly she saw why he delighted so in making her blush, because when she saw that brick red rise up from his neck and suffuse his cheeks, she felt gleeful.

"Wednesday?" she asked, shocked at herself.

"I am trying to be a gentleman!"

Of course he was. And it didn't come naturally to him, either. One little push, and he wouldn't be a gentleman at all.

But did she know how to handle that?

"Here's a blanket," he said, sternly, handing it to her.

She glanced down before she took the blanket from him. Plain white, the perfect underwear for the nanny to have her encounter with the billionaire playboy! Of course the encounter was tragic, rather than romantic. She really didn't have what it took to start a fire that she didn't know how to put out!

She wrapped the blanket around herself, lurched off the bed, nearly tripped in the folds.

He reached out to steady her. "It's okay," he said softly. "Don't be embarrassed."

She looked at where his hand rested on her arm. There was that potential for fire again. She pulled her arm away. "I have to go to the bathroom. Now can I be embarrassed?"

"Yeah, okay. Everybody on the planet has to go to the bathroom about four times a day, but if you want to be embarrassed about it be my guest." And then he grinned at her in a way that made embarrassment ease instead of grow worse, because when he grinned like that she saw the person he *really* was.

Not a billionaire playboy riding the helm of a very successful company. Not the owner of a grand apartment, and the pilot of his own airplane.

The kid in the picture on the beach, long ago.

And in her wildest fantasies, she could see herself sitting around a campfire, wrapped in a blanket like this one, her children shoulder to shoulder with her, saying,

"Tell us again how you met Daddy."

She bolted out of the cabin, then took her time trying to regain her composure. Finally she went back in.

He had pulled the couch in front of the fire and patted the place beside him. "Nice and warm."

Cottage. Fire. Gorgeous man.

In anyone else's life this would be a good equation! She squeezed herself into the far corner of the couch, as far away from him as she could get.

He passed her half a chocolate bar.

She swore quietly. Cottage. Fire. Gorgeous man. Chocolate.

"Nannys aren't allowed to swear," he reprimanded her lightly.

"Under duress!"

"What kind of duress?" he asked innocently.

She closed her eyes. *Don't tell him, idiot.* Naturally her mouth started moving before it received the strict instructions from her brain to shut up. "You'll probably think this is hilarious, but I'm finding you very attractive."

At least it wasn't a declaration of love.

"It's probably a symptom of getting too cold," she added in a rush. "Lack of oxygen to the brain. Or something."

"It's probably the way I look in a blanket," he said, deadpan.

"I suppose there is that," she agreed reluctantly, and then with a certain desperation, "Is there any more chocolate?"

"I find you attractive, too, Dannie."

She blew out a disbelieving snort.

He leaned across the distance between them and touched her hair. "I can't tell you how long I've wanted to do this." His hands stroked her hair, his fingers a comb going through the tangles gently pulling them free. He moved closer to her, buried his face in her hair, inhaled.

She was so aware this was his game, his territory, he *knew* just how to make a woman melt. Spineless creature that she was, she didn't care. In her mind she took that stupid locket and threw it way out into Moose Lake.

What kind of fire she could or could not put out suddenly didn't matter. So close to him, so engulfed in the sensation of his hands claiming her hair, she didn't care if she burned up on the fires of passion!

She turned her head, caught the side of his lip, touched it with her tongue. He froze, leaned back, stared at her, golden light from the fire flickering across the handsome features of his face.

And then he surrendered. Only it was not a surrender at all. He met her tentativeness with boldness that took her breath away. He plundered her lips, took them captive, tasted them with hunger and welcome.

She knew then the totality of the lie she had told herself about loving another, about pining for another.

Because she had never felt this intensity of feeling before, as if fireworks were exploding against a night sky, as if her heart had started to beat after a long slumber, as if her blood had turned to fire. There was not a remnant of cold left in her.

Burn, she told herself blissfully, *burn.*

"I've wanted to do that for a long time, too," he whispered, his voice sexy, low and hoarse. "You taste of rain. Your hair smells of flowers, you do not disappoint, Danielle."

She tasted him, rubbed her lips over the raspiness of whiskers, back to the softness of his mouth, along the column of his neck. She gave herself permission to let go.

And felt the exquisite pull of complete freedom. She went back to his mouth, greedy for his taste and for the sensation of him. She let her hands roam his bare skin, felt the exquisite texture of it, soft, the hardness of male muscle and bone just beneath that surface softness.

His breathing was coming in hard gasps, almost as if she knew what she was doing.

She both did and didn't. The part of her that was knowledge knew nothing of this, she was an explorer in unmapped terrain. But the part of her that was instinct, animal and primal, knew everything about this, knew just how to make him crazy.

She loved it when she felt him begin to tremble as

her lips followed the path scorched out first across his naked chest with her hand.

"Stop," he said hoarsely.

She laughed, loving this new wicked side to herself. "No."

But he pulled away from her, back to his own side of the couch. As she watched him with narrowed eyes, he ran a hand through the spikiness of his hair that looked bronze in the firelight.

"We aren't doing this," he said, low in his throat, not looking at her.

She laughed again, feeling the exquisiteness of her power.

"I'm not kidding, Dannie. My sister would kill me."

"You're going to mention your sister *now?*"

"She always comes to mind when I'm trying to do the decent thing," he said sourly.

"I'm a grown woman," she said. "I make my own decisions."

"Yeah, good ones, like following me into the water when it was completely unnecessary." She moved across the couch toward him. He leaped out of it.

"Dannie, don't make this hard on me."

"I plan to make it very hard on you," she said dangerously, gathering her own blanket around her, sliding off the couch.

"Hey, I hear something."

She smiled. "Sure you do."

"It's a powerboat!"

She froze, tilted her head, could not believe the stinginess of the gods. They were stealing her moment from her! She had *chosen* to burn.

And now the choice was being taken away from her! There was no missing his expression of relief as the sound of the motor grew louder out there in the darkness. With one last look at her—gratitude over a near miss, wistful, too, he grabbed his blanket tighter with one fist, and bolted out the door.

As soon as he was gone, the feeling of power left her with a slam. She flopped back on the couch and contemplated what had just transpired.

She, Danielle Springer, had become the tigress.

"Shameless hussy, more like," she told herself.

She was not being rescued in a blanket! Her state of undress suddenly felt like a neon Shameless Hussy sign! She tossed it down and grabbed her jeans from where he had hung them on a line beside the fire.

They were only marginally drier than before, and now beginning to stiffen as if someone had accidentally dropped a box of starch in with the laundry.

Nonetheless, she lay back down on the bed and tried valiantly to squeeze them back on.

She had just gotten to that awful hip part when he came back in the door.

"Don't look," she said huffily. "I'm getting dressed. I plan to maintain my dignity." As if it wasn't way too late for that!

He made a noise she didn't like.

She let go of her jeans and rolled up on her elbow to look at him. "What?"

"That was Michael in the boat. The bottom of the lake is really rocky here and he can't see because it's too dark. He said if we'd be okay for the night, he'd come back in the morning."

"And you told him we'd be okay for the night?" she said incredulously. It was so obvious things were not okay, that her self-discipline had unraveled like a spool of yarn beneath the claws of a determined kitten.

"That's what I told him."

"Without asking me?"

"Sorry, I'm used to making executive decisions."

She picked up a pillow and hurled it at him. He ducked. She hurled every pillow on that bed, and didn't hit him once. If there had been anything else to pick up and throw, she would have done that, too.

But there was nothing left, not within reach, and she was not going to get up with her jeans half on and half off to go searching. Instead she picked up her discarded blanket, and pulled it over herself, even over her head.

"Go away," she said, muffled.

It occurred to her, her thirty seconds of passion had done the worst possible thing: turned her into her parents! Loss of control happened that fast.

And had such dire consequences, too. Look at her mom and dad. A perfect example of people prepared to burn in the name of love.

She peeked up from the blanket.

In the murky darkness of the cabin, she saw he had not gone away completely. He had found a stub of a candle and lit it. Now he was going through the rough cabinets, pulling out cans.

"You want something to eat?" he asked, as if she hadn't just been a complete shrew, made a complete fool of herself.

Of course she wanted something to eat! That's how she handled pain. That's why the jeans didn't fit in the first place. She yanked them back off, wrapped herself tightly in the blanket and crossed the room to him. If he could pretend nothing had happened, so could she.

"This looks good," she said, picking up a can of tinned spaghetti. If he noticed her enthusiasm was forced, he didn't say a word.

"Delicious," he agreed, looking everywhere but at her, as if somehow spaghetti was forbidden food, like the apple in the garden of Eden.

CHAPTER SEVEN

"Delicious," Dannie said woodenly. "Thank you for preparing dinner."

Hell hath no fury like a woman scorned, Joshua thought, trying not to look at Dannie. He'd been right about her and spaghetti. Her mouth formed the most delectable little *O* as she sucked it back. No twisting the spaghetti around her fork using a spoon for her.

The ancient stove in the cabin was propane fired, and either the tanks had not been filled, because there was going to be no season this year at Moose Lake, or it had just given out in old age. He'd tried his luck with a frying pan and a pot over the fire, and the result was about as far from delicious as he could have made it. Even on purpose.

"Everything's scorched," he pointed out.

Something flashed in her eyes, vulnerable, and then closed up again. Truthfully it wouldn't have mattered if it was lobster tails and truffles. Everything he put in his mouth tasted like sawdust. Burnt sawdust.

The world was tasteless because he'd hurt her. Insulted her. Rejected her.

It was for her own bloody good! And if she didn't quit doing that to the spaghetti his resolve would melt like sugar in boiling water.

He made the mistake of looking at her, her features softened by the golden light of the fire and the tiny, guttering candles, but her expression hardened into indifference and he could see straight through to the hurt that lay underneath.

She plucked a noodle from her bowl, and he felt that surge of heat, of pure wanting. He knew himself. Part of it was because she was such a good girl, prim and prissy, a bit of a plain Jane.

It was the librarian fantasy, where a beautiful hellcat lurked just under the surface of the mask of respectability.

Except that part wasn't a fantasy. Unleashed, Danielle Springer was a hellcat! And the beauty part just deepened and deepened and deepened.

He wanted back what he had lost. Not the heated kisses; he'd had plenty of those and would have plenty more.

No, what he wanted back was the rare trust he felt for her and had gained from her. What he wanted back was the ease that had developed between them over the past few days, the sense of companionship.

"Want to play cards?" he asked her.

The look she gave him could have wilted newly budded roses. "No, thanks."

"Charades?"

No answer.

"Do you want dessert?"

The faintest glimmer of interest that was quickly doused.

"It's going to be a long evening, Dannie."

"God forbid you should ever be bored."

"As if anybody could ever be bored around you," he muttered. "Aggravating, annoying, doesn't listen, doesn't appreciate when sacrifices have been made for her own good—"

She cut him off. "What were the dessert options?"

"Chocolate cake. No oven, but chocolate cake." Just to get away from the condemnation in her eyes, he got up, his blanket held up tightly, and went and looked at the cake mix box he had found in one of the cupboards.

He fumbled around in the poor light until he found another pot, dumped the cake mix in and added water from a container he had filled at the lake. He went and crouched in front of the fire, holding the pot over the embers, stirring, waiting, stirring.

Then he went and got a spoon, and sat on the couch. "You want some?" he asked.

"Sure. The girl who can't even squeeze into her jeans will forgive anything for cake," she said. "Even bad cake. Fried cake. I bet it's gross."

"It isn't," he lied. "You looked great in those jeans. Stop it." And then, cautiously, he said, "What's to forgive?"

"I wanted to keep kissing. You didn't."

"I need a friend more than I need someone to kiss. Do you know how fast things can blow up when people go there?" He almost added *before they're ready*. But that implied he was going to be ready someday, and he wasn't sure that was true. You couldn't say things to Dannie Springer until you were sure they were true.

Silence.

"Come on," he said softly. "Forgive me. Come eat cake." He wasn't aware his heart had stopped beating until it started again when she flopped down on the couch beside him.

He filled up the spoon with goo and passed it to her, tried not to look at how her lips closed around that spoon. Then he looked anyway, feeling regret and yearning in equal amounts. He'd thought watching her eat spaghetti was sexy? The girl made sharing a spoon seem like something out of the *Kama Sutra*.

The cake was like a horrible, soggy pudding with lumps in it, but they ate it all, passing the spoon back and forth, and it tasted to him of ambrosia.

"Tell me something about you that no one knows," he invited her, wanting that trust back, longing for the intimacy they had shared on the lakeshore. Even if it had been dangerous. It couldn't be any more dangerous than sharing a spoon with her. "Just one thing."

"Is that one of your playboy lines?" she asked.

"No." And it was true. He had never said that to a single person before.

Still, she seemed suspicious and probably rightly so. "You first."

When I put that spoon in my mouth, all I can think is that it has been in your mouth first.

"I was a ninety-pound weakling up until the tenth grade."

"I already knew that. Your sister has a picture of you."

"Out where anyone can see it?" he asked, pretending to be galled.

"Probably posted on the Internet," she said. "Try again."

There was one thing no one knew about him, and for a moment it rose up in him begging to be released. To her. For a moment, the thought of not carrying that burden anymore was intoxicating in its temptation.

"Sometimes I pass gas in elevators," he said, trying for a light note, trying to be superficial and funny and irreverent, trying to fight the demon that wanted out.

"You do not! That's gross."

"Real men often are," he said. "You heard it here first."

"Wow. I don't even think I want to kiss you again."

"That's good."

"Was it that terrible?" she demanded.

Could she really believe it had been terrible? That made the temptation to show her almost too great to bear. Instead, he gnawed on the now empty spoon. "No," he said gruffly, "It wasn't terrible at all. Your turn."

"Um, in ninth grade I sent Leonard Burnside a rose. I put that it was from Miss Marchand, the French teacher."

"You liked him?"

"Hated him," she said. "Full-of-himself jock. He actually went to the library and learned a phrase in French that he tried out on her. Got kicked out of school for three days."

"Note to self—do not get on Danielle Springer's bad side."

"I never told anyone. It was such a guilty pleasure. Your turn."

"I don't floss, ever."

"You *are* gross."

"You mean you could tell I didn't floss?" he asked sulkily. "I knew if you really knew me, you wouldn't want to kiss me."

And then the best thing happened. She was laughing. And he was laughing. And they were planning cruel sequences that she could have played on full-of-himself Lennie Burnside.

It grew very quiet. The fire sputtered, and he felt warm and content, drowsy. She shifted over, he felt her head fall onto his shoulder. Even though he knew better, he reached out and fiddled with her hair.

"The part I don't get about you," she said, after a long time that made him wonder if she'd spent all that time thinking of him, "is if you had such a good time with your family on family holidays, why is your own company geared to the young and restless crowd?"

The battle within him was surprisingly short. He had carried it long enough. The burden was too heavy.

He was shocked that he *wanted* to tell her. And only her.

Shocked that he wanted her to know him completely. With all his flaws and with all his weaknesses. He wanted her to know he was a man capable of making dreadful errors. He wanted to know if the unvarnished truth about him would douse that look in her eyes when she looked at him, dewy, yearning.

"When I was in college," he said softly, "the girl I was dating became pregnant. We had a son. We agreed to put him up for adoption."

For a long time she was absolutely silent, and then she looked at him. In the faint light of the fire, it was as if she was unmasked.

What he saw in her eyes was not condemnation. Or anything close to it.

Love.

Her hand touched his face, stroked, comforting.

"You didn't want to," Dannie guessed softly. "Oh, Joshua."

He glanced at her through the golden light of the dying fire. She was looking at him intently, as if she was holding her breath. Her hand was still on his cheek. He could turn his head just a touch and nibble her thumb. But it would be wrong. A lie. Trying to distract them both from the real intimacy that was happening here, and from her deepest secret, which he had just seen in her eyes.

"No, I didn't want to. I guess I wanted what I'd had before, a family to call my own again, that *feeling*. I cannot tell you how I missed that feeling after Mom and Dad died. Of belonging, of having a place to go to where people knew you, clean through. Of being held to a certain standard by the people who knew you best and knew what you were capable of."

He was shocked by how much he had said, and also shocked by how easily the words came, as if all these years they had just waited below the surface to be given voice.

"What happened to the baby?" Dannie asked quietly.

"Sarah didn't want to be tied down. She wasn't ready to settle down. I considered, briefly, trying to go it on my own, as a single dad, but Sarah thought that was stupid. A single dad, just starting in life, when all these established families who could give that baby so much stability and love were just waiting to adopt? My head agreed with her. My heart—"

He stopped, composing himself, while she did the perfect thing and said nothing. He went on, "My heart never did. Some men could be unchanged by that. I wasn't. I couldn't even finish school. I tried to run away from what I was feeling. I had abandoned my own son to the keeping of strangers. What kind of person did a thing like that?

"I traveled the world and developed an aversion for places that catered to families. Wasn't there anywhere a guy like me could get away from all that love? I kind of just fell into the resort business, bought a rundown hotel in Italy, started catering to the young and hip and single, and became a runaway success before I knew what had hit me."

Her hand, where it touched his cheek, was tender. It felt like absolution. But he knew the truth. She could not absolve him.

Silence for a long, long time.

And then she said, "Funny, that your company is called Sun. If you say it, instead of spell it, it's kind of like you carried him with you, isn't it? Your son. Into every single day."

That was the problem with showing your heart to someone like Dannie. She saw it so clearly.

And then she said, "Have you considered the possibility that what you did was best for him? That he did get a family who were desperate for a child to love? Who could give him exactly what you missed so much after your parents died?"

"On those rare occasions that I allow myself to think about it, that is my hope. No, more than a hope. A prayer. And I'm a man who doesn't pray much, Dannie."

"Have you ever thought of finding him?" she asked softly.

"Now and then."

"And what stops you?"

"How complicated it all seems. Just go on the Internet and type in *adoption* to see what a mess of options there are, red tape, legal ramifications, ethical dilemmas."

Dannie wasn't buying it, seeing straight through him. "You must have a team of lawyers who could cut to the quick in about ten minutes. If you haven't done it, there's another reason."

"Fear, then, I guess," he said, relieved to make his

truth complete, wanting her to know who he really was. Maybe wanting himself to know, too. "Fear of being rejected. Fear of opening up a wanting that will never be satisfied, searching the earth for what I can't have or can't find."

"Oh, Joshua," she said sadly, "you don't get it at all, do you?"

"I don't?" He had told her his deepest truth, and though the light of love that shone in her eyes did not lessen, her words made him feel the arrow of her disappointment.

A woman like Dannie could show a man who was lost how to find his way home. Like being in a family, she would never accept anything but his best. Like being in a family, she would show him how to get there when he couldn't find his way by himself.

For the first time in a very, very long time, the sense of loneliness within him eased, the sense that no one really knew him dissipated.

"When you gave your son up for adoption, it wasn't really about what you needed or wanted, Joshua," she said gently. "And it isn't now, either. It's about what he needs and wants. What if he wants to know who his biological father is?"

And suddenly he saw how terribly self-centered he had always been. He had become more so, not less, after he had walked away from his baby seven years ago. He had layered himself in self-protective self-centeredness.

And he was so glad he had not taken that kiss with Dannie to where it wanted to go.

Because he had things he needed to do, roads he needed to travel down, places he needed to visit. Places of the heart.

For a moment, sitting here by the fire, exchanging

laughter and confidences, eating off the same spoon, slurping spaghetti, he had thought it felt like home-coming.

Now he saw he could not have that feeling, not with her and not with anyone else, not until he had made peace with who he was and what he had done.

A long time ago he had given his own flesh and blood into the keeping of strangers. He had tried to convince himself it was the right decision. He had ra-tionalized all the reasons it was okay. But in the back of his mind, he had still been a man, self-centered and egotistical, *knowing* that child would have disrupted his plans and his life and his dreams.

Ironically, even after he'd made the decision that would supposedly set him free, he had been a prisoner of it.

Dannie had seen that right away. *Sun. Son.*

A nibbling sense of failure, of having made a mistake in an area where it really counted, had chased him, and chased him hard. He had barely paused to catch a breath at each of his successes before beginning to run again. He had lost faith in himself because of that decision.

And no amount of success, money, power or acqui-sition had ever absolved him.

But Dannie was right. It was about the child, not about him. If he found out if his boy was okay, then would the demons rest? If he was able to put the needs of that babe ahead of his own, then was he the man worthy of what he saw in Dannie's eyes?

Joshua realized when he had come back into this cabin, after Michael had roared away in the motorboat, leaving them here together until morning, he had thought his mission was to get her to trust him again, the way she had when she had told him about her disastrous nonrelationship with the college professor. The way she had when she had told him about a wedding gown that she had spent all her money on and that she would never wear.

But now he saw that mission for what it was: impossible.

He could not ask anyone else to place their trust in him until he had restored his trust in himself, his belief that he could be counted on to do the right thing.

Where did that start? Maybe his journey had begun already, with saying yes to the needs of his niece and nephew. And then again, maybe that didn't count, since he'd had an ulterior motive.

Maybe his journey had begun when he had backed away from Dannie, backed away from the soft invitation of her lips and the hot invitation of her eyes, because he had known he was not ready and neither was she.

And maybe he could win back his trust in himself by taking one tiny step at a time. Was it as simple—and as difficult—as adding his name to an adoption registry, so that his son would know if he ever wanted him, he would be there for him?

"Thank you for trusting me," Dannie said softly.

The last of the embers were dying, and her voice came at him out of the darkness.

"Dannie, you are completely trustworthy," he said. And he wondered if someday he was going to be a man worthy of that.

But he had a lot of work to do before he was. The darkness claimed him, and when he woke in the morning, it was to the sound of a powerboat moving across the lake. His neck hurt from sleeping on the couch; he could not believe how good it felt to have her cuddled into him.

Trusting.

He sighed, put her away from him, got up and pulled his stiff slacks from where they were strung in front of the now-dead fire.

Trust. He could not even trust himself to look at her, did not think he was strong enough to fight the desire to say good morning to her with a kiss.

Dannie barely spoke on the way back across the water. Neither did he. There was something so deep between them now it didn't even need words. That was what he wanted to be worthy of.

They had barely landed when Susie greeted them, by dancing between the two of them, and throwing her sturdy arms around their knees, screeching as if it was Christmas morning. Even the baby seemed thrilled to see them.

Worthy of this kind of love.

"Were you okay over there?" Sally asked. "What a terrible thing to happen."

"We were fine, but I think the canoe is beyond repair," Joshua said. "I'll replace it."

Sally made a noise that sounded suspiciously close to disgust. "I'm not worried about *stuff,*" she said annoyed. "Stuff can be replaced. People can't."

A little boy in a blue blanket. Never replaced. Not with all the stuff.

"I've made a farewell breakfast," Sally said, turning away from them and leading the way back to the lodge. "Come."

With Susie holding his one hand, as if he completely deserved her love and devotion, and the baby in the crook of his arm, he followed Sally up to the lodge. Dannie trailed behind, lost in her own thoughts.

Sally had made a wonderful feast: bacon, eggs,

pancakes, fresh-squeezed juice. For them. For people she barely knew. Still, she looked a little sad and Joshua realized that was part of the magic of this place. It made everyone who came here into family, it made every farewell difficult.

He had not once discussed business with Michael, and suddenly he was glad. He had not made any promises he could not keep.

Trust. It was time to be a man he could be proud of. That Dannie would be proud of. That maybe his son would be proud of one day.

"I have a confession to make," he said, when the remnants of breakfast had been cleared away. Susie was in front of the fire, playing with an old wooden fire engine, out of earshot.

He looked Michael in the eye. "Michael, I was trying to get rid of my niece and nephew when you called. They'd arrived in my life because of an error in dates. I didn't want them there. They made me feel inadequate and uncomfortable. But when I got the feeling that they might improve my chances of acquiring the lodge, I jumped at your invitation and I brought them with me. I was going to play devoted uncle to manipulate your impressions of me."

He glanced at Dannie, could not read the expression on her face. Had he disappointed her again?

"Instead of *using* them, as I'd intended," he continued, "the lodge gave me a chance to spend time with them and really enjoy them, and I'm very thankful to you and Sally for that opportunity."

No one looked at all surprised by his confession, as if he had been totally transparent all along. No one looked angry or betrayed or hurt.

Somehow he had stumbled on the place that was *family*, where everyone saw you as you were, and while they hoped the best for you, always saw the potential, they never seemed to judge where you were at in this moment.

"So, Joshua, what are your plans for the lodge if you acquire it?" Michael asked, but his voice conveyed a certain reluctance to discuss business.

Joshua was silent. Then he said words he did not think he had said in his entire business career. "I thought I knew. But I don't. I can't make you any promises. I don't know what direction Sun is moving in."

He glanced at Dannie. He knew she had heard the truth. It was not about Sun right now. It was about son.

Michael sighed and looked at his hands, Joshua could clearly see he was a man with the weight of the world on his shoulders.

Dannie, always intuitive, saw it, too.

"Why are you selling Moose Lake Lodge?" Dannie asked. "You obviously love this place so much. To be frank, I can't even picture the place without you two here."

It was the kind of question Joshua would never have asked in the past. It was the kind of question that blurred the lines between professional and personal.

On the other hand, hadn't those lines been blurring for days now? He felt grateful it had been asked. He felt as if the right decision on his part needed the full story and all the facts.

Sally shot Joshua a look, clearly wondering if he would use any weakness against them. She glanced at her husband. He shrugged, and she covered his big work-worn hand with hers.

It was a gesture of such tenderness, some connection between them so strong and so bright, that Joshua felt his eyes smart.

Or maybe it was just from the fire smoking in the

hearth. Or from several days so far out of his element. Or from falling in love with Dannie Springer.

He looked at her again, saw her watching Sally with such enormous compassion. Remembered her over the past few days, laughing, playing with the kids, running into the lake right behind him when the boat had broken free.

A woman a man could share the burdens with, just as Sally and Michael so obviously had shared theirs over the years. A woman a man could go to as himself, flawed, and still feel valued. *Worthy.*

He had said it in his own mind. He was falling in love with her. He waited for the terror to come.

But it didn't. Instead what came was a sense of peace such as he had not felt for a very long time.

"We're selling, or trying to sell, for a number of reasons," Sally said, her voice soft with emotion. "Partly that we're too old to do the place justice anymore." She stopped, distressed, and he watched Michael's hand tighten over hers.

"It's mostly that our daughter is sick," Michael said gruffly. "Darlene has an aggressive form of a degenerative muscle disorder. She practically grew up here, but she can't come here anymore. She's got three little kids and she's a single mom.

"Pretty soon she's going to need a wheelchair. And if she's going to stay in her own home, everything has to be changed, from the cabinets to the door handles. She's going to need a special lift system to get in the bathtub. She's going to need a modified van. She's going to need us."

Joshua heard the unspoken: it was going to take more money than they knew how to raise to take care of their daughter as her health deteriorated.

Michael got up abruptly and walked out into the clear brightness of the morning, a man prepared to do the right thing, no matter how hard it was, no matter what it cost him, no matter what he had to let go of.

"Sorry," Sally said, watching him go, pain and love equal in her eyes. "It's hard for a man to care as much as he does and to find himself helpless."

It really confirmed everything Joshua already knew about love. It could slay the strongest man. It could tear the flesh from his bones. It could leave him trembling and unsure of the world.

He looked at Dannie. She was staring into the fire.

He saw her hand had crept into Sally's. Such a small thing. Such a right thing.

He felt sick to his stomach. He wanted the Moose Lake Lodge, and he wanted it badly. But he wasn't going to take advantage of these fine people's misery.

Except they needed the money.

And they only had one way to get it.

To sell what they loved most. Their history. Their memories.

Why did his whole life feel all wrong ever since the nanny had put in an appearance?

Only a few days ago, Joshua Cole had been sure of his identity: businessman, entrepreneur. Maybe he'd even embraced the playboy part of it a little bit because it had allowed him to fill up his life with superficial fun but never required anything *real* of him.

Today he was sure of nothing at all, least of all his identity.

Later that morning, his bags packed beside him, Joshua watched Dannie and the kids from the safety of the porch on Angel's Rest. They were walking the beach one last time with Sally, Dannie carrying the baby, her feet bare in the cold sand. He acutely felt, watching that scene, the emptiness of his own life.

He had filled it with stuff instead of substance.

He watched Dannie pull something from her pocket. He saw her reach inside herself for strength, and then she sent that small object hurtling out into the water, further than he could have imagined she could throw.

He saw the glint of gold catching in the sun, before the object completed its upward arch and then plummeted to the lake and slipped beneath the surface with nary a ripple.

From here he could hear Dannie's laughter. And understood that she was free.

He was glad to get on the plane an hour later. His world. Precision. Control. He hoped for freedom as great as he had heard in Dannie's laughter.

But instead of feeling a joyous release as the plane took off, he was acutely aware there would be no more running. He could not fly away from the truths he had to face. They would just be waiting when he landed.

It occurred to him that maybe he would never find his own son. Or maybe he would find him, and the family would choose not to have contact.

But he was aware that he could reclaim his faith in himself in other ways.

Joshua Cole knew his heart was ready.

And he was surprised to find he did have a simple faith, after all. It was that once a heart was ready, the opportunities would come. And once a man was ready, he would take them.

CHAPTER EIGHT

THEY were saying goodbye. Dannie couldn't believe it had happened this fast. She had wanted to tell Joshua she admired him for telling Sally and Michael the truth. She wanted to ask him how he planned to help them, for surely he did.

And she had wanted to thank him for telling her about his son.

But somehow, during that short flight back to Vancouver from Moose Lake Lodge, the opportunity had never come. Aside from the fact his expression had been remote and focused, not inviting any kind of conversation, Jake had been terribly fussy.

Susie had a delayed reaction to the fact they had left her for the night without consulting her, and her upset had intensified when she had not been able to find Michael to tell him goodbye.

Now she was behaving outrageously. Bits of stuffing from the teddy bear Joshua had given her on their first day with him was soon floating in the air, landing in handfuls in the front seats of the aircraft.

Joshua didn't even seem to notice, but no wonder when he landed, he asked them to wait, and then disappeared into the terminal.

When he came back out he told them he had arranged their flight home. A chartered plane would take them to Toronto, a car and driver would meet them and take them to his sister's house.

He took Dannie's hands in both his own. For a moment she thought he was going to kiss her, but he didn't. In some ways the look in his eyes was better than a kiss.

Trusting. Forthright.

"I'll be in touch as soon as I can," he said. "I have some things I need to look after first. I don't know how long it will take, but when it is done, I promise, I will come for you."

Words eerily like those Brent had spoken.

Would she do it again? Build a fantasy around a few words, a vague promise? But when she returned his look, she found herself believing. This time it was real.

But the lifestyles-of-the-rich-and-famous flight home, the growing geographical distance between them, played with her mind. Nothing about this private plane ride seemed *real.*

Was it possible Joshua Cole had divested her from his life?

Was it possible he had left the story in the middle? Was it possible Dannie might never know what happened to Sally and Michael? To Sun and Moose Lake Lodge?

Was it possible he would make that journey of the heart, his decisions about his son, alone? By himself?

He was the playboy. Lethally charming. Had she fallen, hook, line and sinker, for that lethal charm, or had she really seen the genuine Joshua Cole, the one he showed no one else?

Melanie and Ryan arrived home a day later, tanned and relaxed, more in love than ever.

Their affection and respect for each other seemed, impossibly, to have deepened. Susie's behavioral problems evaporated instantly once her secure family unit was back the way she wanted it to be.

Dannie had never felt on the outside of that family quite so much. She had never felt so uncertain of her own choices.

Part of her waited, on pins and needles, jumping every time the phone rang. Because when she thought back on her time with Joshua, it seemed as if it had been exquisitely solid, an island in the land of mist that her life had been. It seemed as if those days at Moose Lake Lodge might have been the most real thing about her entire life.

It felt as if what she had been when she was with him, alive and strong and connected to life, had been the genuine deal. She was sure he had felt it, too.

He had shared his secret self with her. He had told her about his son. Every time she thought of the way he had looked as he told that story, lost and forlorn, and yet so brave and so determined, she felt like weeping. She felt as if she wanted to be there for him as he took the next steps, whatever he decided those would be.

She had been sure he would call. Positive that his promise meant something. She had felt as if he needed her to navigate the waters he was entering, as if she could be on his team as surely as when they had paddled the canoe together.

When he did not call, for one day and then another, her self-doubt returned in force. When a week passed with no call, Dannie condemned herself as the woman who could spin a romance, a fantasy out of the flimsiest of fabrics.

Brent had given her a locket with his picture in it. He had made vague promises. Naturally he was coming home to marry her.

Joshua Cole, World's Sexiest Bachelor, in a moment of complete vulnerability had told her his deepest secret. Naturally that meant he was throwing over all the women he'd been paired with in the past!

He was giving up actresses and singers and heiresses for the nanny! Of course he was! Dannie even took her wedding dress out of its wrapper and laid it on her bed, allowed herself to look at it wistfully and imagine herself gliding down the aisle, *him* waiting for her.

But as the days passed and it became increasingly apparent he wasn't, Dannie found comfort in chocolate rather than her wedding dress!

"Okay," Mel said finally. "Tell me what on earth happened to you, Dannie?"

"What do you mean?"

"You're gaining about a pound a day! You're not the same with the children as you were before. It's as if you've decided to be an employee instead of a member of our family. I miss you! What's going on?"

"It's the whole Brent thing," Dannie lied. *The whole romance thing. The whole life thing.*

But Melanie stared at her, and understanding, totally unwanted, dawned in her eyes.

"It's not Brent," she guessed softly. "It's my brother. What has Josh done to you?"

"Nothing," Dannie said, quickly. Obviously way too quickly.

"I'm going to kill him," Mel said.

Dannie had a sudden humiliating picture of Mel phoning her brother and reaming him out for having done something to her nanny.

The one he had probably forgotten existed as soon as he'd divested himself of her at the airport!

"You didn't do a bit of matchmaking, did you? You

didn't think your brother and I would make a good pair, did you?" Dannie asked, remembering Joshua's embarrassing conclusion on their first meeting.

"Of course not," Melanie said quickly and vehemently, her eyes sliding all over the place and landing everywhere but on her nanny's face.

"You did!" Dannie breathed.

"I didn't. I mean not officially."

"But unofficially?"

"Oh, Dannie, I just love you so. And him. And you both seemed so lonely and so lost and so devoted to making absolutely the wrong choices for yourselves. I thought it couldn't hurt to put you together and just see what happened. I thought it couldn't do any harm. But it did, didn't it?"

Harm? Dannie thought of her days with Joshua, of the delight of getting to know him, and herself. Even if he never called, could those days be taken away from her? Could what she had glimpsed in herself fade away?

Only if she let it.

"I'm going to kill him," Melanie said again, but with no real force.

"You know what, Melanie?" Dannie said slowly, as understanding dawned in her. "Your brother didn't do anything to me. I do things to myself."

"What does that mean?" Melanie asked, skeptical.

"It means I have an imagination that fills in the gaps where reality leaves off."

As she said it, Dannie's understanding of herself grew. She was too willing to give her emotions into the keeping of other people. She was too willing to rearrange her whole world around a possibility, to put her whole life on hold while she *waited* for someone else to call the shots.

It was not admirable that she was willing to put her whole world and her whole life on hold in anticipation of some great love, some great event in the future! She'd done it with Brent on very little evidence, and now on even less evidence—only four days—she was going to waste time mooning over Joshua Cole?

No, he could have his car and his airplane and his fancy apartment and his five-star resorts. He could have heiresses and actresses and rock stars, if that was what made him happy. Love wanted the beloved to be happy. It didn't demand ownership!

Besides, Dannie missed the girl she had been, ever so briefly, in that canoe. Not a girl who *waited* for life to happen, but someone who participated fully, someone who had discovered her own strength and insisted on pulling her own weight.

While Melanie watched her, Dannie took the ice cream she was eating and washed it down the sink.

"That's it," she told her friend and employer. "No more self-pity. No more being victimized. I have a life to live!"

"I'm still going to kill him," Melanie muttered.

"Not for my benefit, you're not," Dannie said firmly.

The next day, her day off, she took the wedding gown to a local theatrical company and donated it to their costume department. They were thrilled to have it, and frankly she was thrilled to see it go. That's where that fantasy concoction of silk and lace belonged, in a world of make-believe. And that's where she was living no longer.

And then she went and signed up for canoe lessons at a place called Wilderness Ways Center. And while she was there, she noticed they had a class in rock climbing, and their own rock wall, so she signed up for that, too.

She took to her activities intensively, spending every free minute at the centre.

The loveliest and most unexpected thing happened. Danielle Springer had been waiting her whole life to fall in love. And she did.

She fell in love with herself.

She fell in love with the laughter-filled woman who attacked climbing walls and finicky canoes with a complete sense of adventure. She fell in love with the woman, whom she recognized had always been afraid of life, suddenly embracing its uncertainties.

She had always been a good nanny, and she knew that, but suddenly she felt as if she was a great nanny, because she was passing on this new and incredible sense of adventure and discovery to the children.

As the cool, fresh days of spring turned to the hot, humid days of summer, she found herself right out there jumping through the sprinkler with Susie, immersed in the wading pool with Jake.

She was teaching her young charges what she was learning: that life was a gift. An imperfect life, a life that did not go as planned, was no less a gift. Maybe a surprising life was even more of one.

The strangest thing was the more she danced with the gypsy spirit she was discovering in herself, the less she needed a man to validate her! When Joshua Cole had touched her lip with his thumb, he had told her he knew something of her that she did not know of herself.

But now she did! She knew she was strong and independent and capable. And fun loving. And full of mischief. And ready to dance with life! The irony, of course, was that men, who had always treated her as invisible, liked her. They flocked to her! They flirted with her.

The phone started ringing for her all the time. Now

that she could have anything she wanted, and anyone, she was surprised how much herself was enough. She liked how uncomplicated it was to live her own life, pursue her own interests, immerse herself in her job and her everyday pleasures. Something as simple as lying on the fragrant back lawn at night looking with wonder at the stars filled her to the top.

She was just coming in the door from her kayak lesson, when Melanie told her she had a phone call.

"It's Joshua," Melanie said, eyebrows raised, not even trying to hide her hope and delight that her brother might be coming to his senses.

Dannie picked up the phone. Despite how she had made herself over, her heart was hammering in her throat.

"How are you?" he asked.

Such a simple question. And yet the sound of his voice, alone, familiar, deep, masculine, tender, made her call him, in her own mind, "beloved."

"I'm fine, Joshua." Before she could ask how he was, he started talking again.

"Mel says you've been keeping really busy. Canoeing and rock climbing."

"I've been staying busy," she said, keeping her voice carefully neutral so he would not hear the unspoken, *I wish you could do it with me.*

"She says the guys are calling there all the time for you."

Was that faint jealousy in the World's Sexiest Bachelor's voice? Dannie laughed. "Not *all* the time."

His voice went very low. "She says you don't go out with any of them. Not on dates, anyway."

"Joshua! Your sister shouldn't be telling you anything about my private life."

"She can't resist me when I beg," he said.

Who could? "Why are you begging for information about me?"

"You know why."

Yes. She said nothing, afraid to speak, afraid to believe, afraid this was a test of all her resolve to not live in her fantasies but to create a dynamic reality for herself in the here and the now.

"Dannie, I couldn't call you until I had looked after certain things. Until I had done my very best to clear away any baggage, any heartache that would have kept me from being the man you deserve."

She wanted to tell him he was wrong, that he had always been the man she deserved, but something in her asked her to wait, to listen, and most of all, to believe.

"When I got back from Moose Lake Lodge, I thought of what you had said, about putting the ball in my son's court. Doing what he needed, instead of what I thought I needed or wanted. I discussed the options with one of my lawyers. After a lot of discussion we finally agreed to register with an agency that specializes in triad reunions. That means all three parties, the child, the adoptive family and the birth parents, have to want a contact or a meeting or a reunion. Until all three pieces are in place, nothing happens."

She could hear the emotion in his voice. She felt so proud of him. She felt as if she had never loved him more.

There was a long, long silence. Finally he spoke, whispered a single word.

"Dannie."

He couldn't possibly be crying. He couldn't. Not the strong, totally in control playboy. Not the World's Sexiest Bachelor. Not one of the world's most successful entrepreneurs and resort visionaries.

Her Joshua, the one she had always seen, while the rest of the world bought the role he was playing, was capable of this great tenderness, this great vulnerability, this final unmasking.

"Dannie," Joshua choked out, "they were waiting for me."

"Oh, Joshua," she breathed his name, and then again in confirmation that he was exactly who she had known he was. "Oh, Joshua."

The tears of joy were coursing down her own cheeks.

"I've spoken to his parents on the phone. And him. It's funny, I had not grieved the death of his mother, until I had to tell him she was gone."

"Joshua." Again his name came from her lips like a celebration, like a prayer.

"I've arranged to meet my son and his adoptive parents this weekend. They live in Calgary. His name's Jared. I—" he stopped, hesitated, his voice still hoarse with emotion "—I'd like you to come with me."

"Why?" she said. It was a hard question to ask, when everything in her just wanted to say *yes*. Scream yes.

But his answer was everything. Everything. If he wanted her to come with him because of her skills as a nanny, it didn't count. It wasn't what she wanted. It wasn't even close. The seconds before he answered were easily the longest of her life.

"I want you to come with me because this is the most important thing I've ever done, and I cannot imagine doing it without you. I want you to come with me because I trust you more than I trust myself," he said, and then softly, ever so softly, "I want you to come because I think I could fall in love with you. I think I'm halfway there, already."

She couldn't speak through the tears.

"Dannie, are you there?"

"Yes."

"Will you?"

The question asked more than whether she would accompany him to meet his son for the first time.

It asked her to take a chance on this crazy, unpredictable, potential-for-heartbreak thing called love all over again.

"Will I? Oh, Joshua, I'm just like them." She took a deep breath. It did not stop her voice from shaking. "I've been waiting for you."

She didn't even know how true that was until she spoke the words. She hadn't even realized all of it—the canoeing and rock climbing, the boldly saying yes to life, all of it had been about being ready.

Being the kind of woman ready to fall in love—sure of herself and her place in the world first.

Not being *needy*, but being strong. Not needing another person to complete her, but bringing her whole self to a union.

It was true, she had been waiting for Joshua. It was just as true that she had been waiting for herself.

CHAPTER NINE

I'VE been waiting for you.

The words, and his memory of them, had been like a lifeline through the past few days. He held on to them, he held on to the beauty of what he had heard in Dannie's voice.

Joshua Cole had been the prime player in million-dollar deals. He had taken a company from nothing and turned it into something. He single-handedly ran an empire valued in billions, not millions.

And yet all that paled in comparison to how he felt about meeting his son. And about seeing Dannie again.

It was as if, in all his world, only two things mattered. Only two things had become important.

And both those things were all about *the* thing. Love.

He waited at the Calgary International airport for Dannie, nervously holding a bouquet of flowers for her. He had purchased flowers for dozens of women, and it had never caused him so much anxiety, choosing each bloom personally, debating over daisies or roses, baby's breath or lily of the valley.

He saw Dannie coming through the door of the security area, and was astonished by the changes in her, knew that daisies were *exactly* right, unpretentious, simple, earthy, beautiful, hardy.

Dannie looked as if she was twenty pounds lighter than she had been the first time he'd seen her. Gone was any vestige of the frumpalumpa. Today she was dressed in a white tailored silk shirt, a blazer, amazing low-riding jeans. He was aware he wouldn't have any problem peeling those jeans off her if they got wet!

Not that he wanted his mind to be going there since he was working so hard at being the man she deserved. Decent. Considerate. Strong. A man of integrity and honor.

Her hair was, thankfully, the same jet-black gypsy tangle. She had made no effort to tame it, and it sprang around her head in sexy, unruly curls that his fingers ached to touch. She was tanned and healthy looking, her turquoise eyes subtly shaded with makeup that made them pop.

He saw the man who came out the door ahead of her glance back, knew enough about male body language to know he was interested.

Hey, buddy, I saw her first.

And that was the truth. He had *seen* her, even before she had done one single thing to be seen.

Joshua saw that though Dannie had always radiated calm, a ship confident of riding out the storm, now there were layers to that calm. He saw the confidence in her. And the purity of her strength. And he knew he had never needed it more.

She saw him, and he didn't think for as long as he lived, he would ever forget the look in her eyes. More than welcome. More than joy. Bigger.

Homecoming.

She flew into his arms, no reservations, and he

picked her up and swung her around, felt his own welcoming answer to the look in her eyes, felt how right her sweet weight was in his arms, as if she belonged there, her softness melting into the firmness of his chest.

Finally, he put her down and gazed at her, silent, wonder filled. He touched her hair, just to make it real.

"Tonight is just you and me," he said, picking up her bag, realizing he couldn't just stand there staring at her forever, even if that's what he wanted to do. "We're going to meet Jared and his mom and dad for lunch tomorrow at their house, and if that goes okay, we're going to go to the zoo."

"How are you doing?" she asked, seeing right through the illusion of control reciting the itinerary was supposed to give him!

He smiled at how she could see right through the confidence of the designer suit, and the take-control businessman attitude.

Just as he had seen her before anyone else had, she had seen him.

"Terrified," he whispered. Not just about Jared, either, but about making a mistake with her. Funny, he who had been classified as a playboy, felt he had no skill at being real. But he needn't have worried.

"What do you want to do tonight?" he asked, his voice faintly strangled.

It sounded hilarious, like a teenage boy fumbling his way through his first date. He felt like a teenage boy, as if he wanted to get this so right. Before her arrival, he'd picked up the newspaper and been scanning it, looking for exactly the activity that would bring them back to the people they had been on that island several weeks ago.

There were a number of live shows in town. Five-star restaurants had been recommended to him. But he had not bought tickets or made reservations because he didn't want it to have that awkward-first-date feeling.

Even though that's probably what it was, he felt way past that.

"Let's order a pizza in the hotel," she said, burying her nose in the bouquet, "and watch a movie in your room."

So simple. So perfect. Like daisies. Like her.

"Um," he actually felt shy, embarrassed. "I booked you a separate room. I didn't think—" He was actually blushing, he could feel it.

She threw back her head and laughed. "You were right, Joshua, you are going to have to woo me. I'm not like the other girls."

"You aren't," he said ruefully. "Not a single soul I know could use the word *woo* seriously like that."

"Well, I intend to be wooed. I'm not just falling into the sack with you."

It was his turn to laugh, to tell the little devil on his shoulder to forget peeling off those pants anytime soon.

That night they sprawled out on his bed in his room, eating pizza and watching movies, and he remembered how it had been that night with her in the cabin.

Exhilarating. But comfortable, too.

At eleven she kissed him good-night, her lips tender and full of promise. But then she went to her own room.

The next morning she insisted they find a rock-climbing wall, because she said the tension was boiling off him.

By the time she'd beaten him to the top of that wall three times, he didn't have any energy left, never mind any tension.

They went shopping together. He was going to buy Jared a teddy bear, but she rolled her eyes at that, and told him seven-year-old boys did not like teddy bears.

Which was a relief, because then he got to look at the really fun stuff like remote control cars and footballs, skateboards and video games. He wanted to buy everything. Dannie, guiding him calmly through the jagged mountain terrain of the heart, told him to choose one.

And so they arrived at Jared's house at lunchtime, he with one remote control car, wishing he had a boxload full of toys to hide behind. He looked at the house, gathering evidence that somehow, despite himself, all those years ago, he had managed to do the right thing.

It was an ordinary house on an ordinary street, well kept, tidy, *loved*. Behind the picket fence, peeping through the leaves of a mature maple tree, he could see a platform in a tree, looking over the yard. A bicycle leaned up against the side of the house. A volleyball lay in the neat grass.

It pleased Joshua more than he could have said that the yard and the house indicated his son had enjoyed an ordinary life, an ordinary family, a life very different than the one Joshua could have given him if he'd hung on instead of letting go.

A better life, he thought, surveying the yard one more time, feeling Dannie's hand tightening in his, a life where everyone had put Jared first. Even the man who had been unaware that he had done so.

Joshua had never in his life been as afraid as he was when he rang that doorbell. A dog barked from inside. A golden retriever, delirious with happiness greeted them first. A lovely woman came to the door, in her early thirties, a redhead with an impish grin and warm green eyes. Behind her stood her husband, as whole-some looking as apple pie, the guy next door who built the tree house and threw the baseballs until dark, and who probably got up predawn to coach the peewee hockey team.

And then the world went still.

Jared ran into the room, all energy and joy. By now, Joshua had seen his son's picture, but it did not prepare him for how he felt. It seemed as if energy streamed off the boy, pure as sunshine. Jared was sturdy, with auburn hair and green eyes that danced with mischief, the confidence of a child who had known only love.

He skidded to a halt, ruffed the dog's ears, gazed at Joshua with intent curiosity.

"You look like me," he decided, "I couldn't really tell from the picture. Hey, Mom, can I get a frog?"

Until that moment, it felt to Joshua as if his life had been a puzzle, the pieces scattered all over the place.

But with those words, *Hey, Mom, can I get a frog* and the sudden laughter that chased the awkwardness from the room, it was as if the pieces drew together and slid firmly into place.

It seemed as if that moment, and all of life, was infused with light, as if, in spite of the efforts of people, rather than because of them, everything had turned out exactly as it was meant to be.

Introductions were made, but they were an odd formality in this group of people that somehow already were, and always would be a family.

The entire weekend, they did nothing special, and yet everything was special. Eating barbecued burgers in the Morgans' backyard, playing Frisbee with the dog, touring the zoo, sitting on the edge of his son's bed, trying to read him a story through the lump in his throat.

Joshua Cole, who had specialized in giving ordinary people spectacular experiences made the humbling discovery that ordinary experiences were made spectacular by the people you shared them with, by the addition of one secret ingredient.

Love.

He discovered that sometimes a man had to work at love.

But most of the time it was just brought to him, even though he might be completely undeserving of it.

"I can't think when I've had a more perfect weekend," Joshua said as he strolled through the airport with Dannie on Sunday night. Her hand in his felt perfect, too.

"Me, neither," she said.

In a few moments, the miles would separate them. How could he make the ache less, take away the sense of loss? Not just for himself, which was the way the old Joshua thought, but for her?

He stopped in front of a jewelry store counter, and they looked at a display of sparkling diamond necklaces together. "Pick one," he said. "Any one. To remember this weekend by."

"No," she said.

"Come on," he said. "To remember me. To show you how much I care for you and am going to miss you until we meet again."

"No," she said, more firmly than the first time.

Too expensive, he thought, not appropriate for their first weekend together, though he had given far more expensive gifts for far less.

"How about one of those, then?" he said, pointing to a glittering display of diamond tennis bracelets.

"Joshua, no!"

"Hey," he said, "I'm wooing you!"

"No," she said, almost gently, as if she was explaining the timetables to a three year old. "That's wowing. There's a difference. I don't need anything to remember this weekend by, Joshua."

"How am I supposed to woo you with an attitude like that?" he asked, pretending to be grouchy.

"For you, Joshua, the easiest thing would be to shower me with gifts, with all the *stuff* money can buy. But that's not what I want. I want the hardest things from you. I want your time. I want your energy. I want you fully engaged. I want *you*. You can't win me by throwing your wealth at me."

He scowled at that. The weekend had gone so well he thought he'd already won her. He could now clearly see that wasn't true.

That she was going to make him work for her heart, and that she planned to give him a run for his money. He could clearly see that he was going to have to win her the old-fashioned way.

And suddenly it felt like the most exciting challenge of his whole life. Better than any of it. Better than buying resorts, better than flying airplanes, better than thrill seeking, better than traveling to the seven wonders of the world.

She was trying to tell him there was no destination. It was all about the trip. And the truth was, he couldn't wait. He felt as if she was leading him to the eighth wonder of the world.

Which existed for each man within the unexplored and unmapped territories of his own heart.

"Dannie," Melanie said, "could you just say yes? My brother is driving me crazy."

They were both standing at her picture window, looking out at the front lawn. Overnight three hundred plastic pink flamingos had appeared on it, splashes of color against the first winter's snow. They spelled out, more or less, DANNIE.

"It's been six months," Melanie said. "He's more insanely in love with you every day. Just say yes."

"I don't really know if the flamingos fit the criteria. He used money."

"He had to have rented them! Or borrowed them. Maybe he even stole them. He didn't buy them. And I bet he was out there himself in the freezing cold spelling your name in tacky plastic birds. If that isn't love, nothing is. Say yes."

"To what?" Dannie said innocently. "He hasn't asked me anything yet."

Dannie smiled at Melanie, allowed herself to feel the tenderness of the flamingos planted in a declaration of love for her. When she had challenged Joshua to woo her, without great displays of wealth and power, nothing could have prepared her for how that man rose to a challenge!

The only exception she had made to her proviso about his using his wealth was plane tickets. Even she had to admit that it was pretty hard to woo someone unless you saw them.

So, he flew to Toronto, and he flew her to Vancouver, or they met in Calgary to have time with Jared and the Morgans.

Melanie was right. Her brother was crazy, but in the most phenomenal way. Never had a woman been wooed the way Danielle Springer was being wooed.

While the weather had still been good, they had attended rock-climbing and canoeing schools together.

To his consternation, Dannie insisted on paying her own tuition. She asked him to donate his offering to the classes Wilderness Ways offered to the Boys & Girls Club.

He had found a guitar—he claimed it had been given to him, so that it was still within her rules of wooing—and sang to her outside his sister's house. He neither knew how to play or how to sing. Listening to him murder a love song had been more endearing than him offering to take her to a concert in Vancouver, which she had said no to, firmly, when he had flashed the very expensive tickets in front of her.

He had made her a cedar chest with his own hands, when she had refused the one he had wanted to buy for her after she had admired it at an antique store they had been browsing through. He didn't know how to build anymore than he knew how to sing, the chest a lopsided testament to his love.

He was slowly filling it with treasures, not a single one that money could buy. The chest held his mother's wedding ring and his grandmother's handmade lace. It held a bronzed baby shoe—his—and a baby picture of Jared. He was giving her his history.

He had made her a locket to replace the one she had thrown away, only his was made out of paper maché and contained his thumb print. She had worn it until it threatened to disintegrate, and then she had put it in the chest with her other treasures.

He had baked her cookies shaped like haphazard hearts and that had tasted strongly of baking soda. One of their most romantic evenings had been over his home-cooked spaghetti, perfecting the art of eating the same noodle, both of them sucking one end of it until their lips met in the middle.

He had sent her dental floss, special delivery, claiming he was a reformed man.

"Is that used?" Melanie had asked, horrified when Danielle had opened the package.

"Never mind," Danielle had said, tucking the envelope in her chest of treasures. "I will show it to my children one day. I will say, 'Your father gave me plaque.'"

"You're as disgusting as him," Melanie griped. "What children? Has he asked you?"

"Not yet."

"He better get on with it. I'm reporting him to the post office if he sends anything else like that."

When he flew in for the weekends, he taught her how to fish on a little canal near Melanie and Ryan's house, and when it froze over, he taught her how to skate. They never caught a single fish, though they caught a frog for Jared, and then had to figure out how to get it to him. Joshua ended up chartering a plane so he didn't have to smuggle the little green creature through airport security.

Dannie never was able to skate without him holding her up, and it just didn't matter. They went for long walks and on star-gazing expeditions. When they passed some children with kittens in a box outside a grocery store, under a huge sign that said Free, he picked out the cutest one for her.

She named it Rhapsody.

When he flew her to Vancouver, she brought him terrible poems that she had written herself, and cooked him disastrous meals. She admired the flowers he was growing for her on his terrace, since he wasn't allowed to buy her anything. They rode the Skytrain, and explored Stanley Park. They spent evenings in the Jacuzzi, in bathing suits.

When they went to Calgary they went on picnics with the Morgans and rode bicycles with Jared on the network of trails. They threw baseballs in the backyard and built a roof on the tree platform so they could sleep out there at night. Joshua proved again he was no builder. That roof leaked like a sieve, which only added to the fun!

They took Jared to the public pools that had waves and waterslides, and they hung out at the libraries that offered story time. They caught bugs for his frog, Simon, and took the golden retriever to obedience class.

Joshua and Jared took ski lessons at the Olympic Park, and she perfected the art of drinking hot chocolate in the ski lodge.

"There he is," Melanie said, looking past the flamingos. She snorted with affection. "The great playboy arrives. If he doesn't ask you this weekend, I'm disowning him."

"You said that last weekend," Dannie reminded her.

"The difference is this weekend I mean it."

"Look, Melanie," Dannie said softly, "he brought you a surprise."

Joshua was getting out of a small sports car, obviously a rental, trying to convince an eight-foot-long toboggan to get out with him. And then a little boy tumbled out of the front seat.

"Ohmygod," Melanie said, and turned wide tear-filled eyes to Dannie. "Is that my nephew?" She didn't wait for an answer, but went out the front door in her sock feet, tripping over pink flamingos in her haste to meet the little boy who looked just like her brother had once looked.

Every day they spent together seemed magical, but that one more so. They took the kids tobogganing, Susie had an instant case of hero-worship for her older cousin.

When they got home, Melanie took the kids under her wing, then handed her brother an envelope. "Enough's enough," she said sternly. "I'll mind the children."

Joshua opened the envelope. Inside it was a map. Danielle could hardly look at him, suddenly shy, wondering if he, too remembered the last time someone had offered to mind the children for them.

They followed the map outside of the city, through the ever deepening darkness and the countryside to a little cabin.

It was inside the cabin that Dannie realized he was in on it. How else could it be completely stocked with tinned spaghetti and boxed cake mix?

He made her a dinner, and then as the fire roared in the stone hearth, he poured the cake mix into a pot, mixed it with water, and cooked it over the fire.

"I don't want any of that," she said.

"Come on. You're just way too skinny."

It was true, but for the first time in her life, she wasn't skinny on purpose. She was skinny because she was so happy there was not a single space in her that food could fill.

Tonight, she thought, looking through the door to the bedroom of the tiny cabin. Tonight would be the night. She leaned forward and kissed him.

Normally he would have kissed her back, but tonight he didn't.

"I can't do it anymore," he said. "I can't kiss you and not have you."

"I know," she said. "It's okay. I'm wooed. Let's go to bed."

"Ah, no."

"What do you mean, no?" she asked stunned.

"Dannie, that's not how an old-fashioned wooing ends."

"It isn't?"

"No," he said and got down on one knee in front of her. "It ends like this." He freed a ring box stuck in his pocket. "Dannie, will you marry me? Will you be mine forever? Will you have my children and be a part of the family that includes my son? And my niece and nephew?"

"Yes," she whispered.

Then he kissed her, but when she tried to get him into that bedroom he wouldn't allow it.

"Nope. You have to wait until the wedding night."

"I do?"

"Yeah."

"Give me the fried cake," she said glumly. She shared the spoon with him. It didn't taste half bad.

"Don't you want to see what's in the box?" he teased.

She'd actually forgotten to look at the ring. The truth was the ring did not mean anything to her. How could it compare to the ring he'd made her out of tinfoil and glue that was in her box of treasures? How could it have the same value as these wonderful days of wooing? Oh, she was going to miss this.

Of course, being married meant it was all going to be replaced. With something better. Much better. She realized she was *starved* for him. For more of him. For his body and for his tongue and for his lips and for his hands all over her.

Her eyes skittered to that bedroom door again. Was he really going to make her wait?

"Open it," he insisted handing her the box.

The lid was very hard to pry open. When she did get it open, she saw why. Instead of a ring, there was a piece of paper folded up to fit in there. Carefully, she unfolded it, tried to understand the legal terms printed on it.

Finally, she got it. Joshua had given her the deed to Moose Lake Lodge.

"I cannot imagine not having you as a full partner in every single thing I do, my confidante, my equal. This is yours, Dannie, to run as you see fit."

She was smiling through her tears.

"How long is it going to take you to plan a wedding?" he asked. "I want you to have it all. The dress, the flower girls, the cathedral, the—"

"No," she said. "No, I don't want any of that. That's all about a wedding, and nothing about a marriage." She began to blush. "Joshua, I can't wait much longer."

"For what?" he said with evil knowing.

"You know."

"Tell me."

So she whispered her secret longings in his ear.

"You're right," he said. "I think we need to do something fast. My honor is at stake. What do you have in mind, then?"

"A quick civil ceremony. As soon as we can get the documents in place."

He laughed. "I forgot you already have a dress."

"I don't," she said. "I'm marrying you in a snowsuit so that we can go straight to our honeymoon."

"You've given that some thought?" he asked, raising a wicked eyebrow at her.

"I'm afraid I have," she confessed, blushing. "I want to have our honeymoon at Moose Lake Lodge at the honeymoon cabin."

"It's snowing up there!" he said.

She smiled. She could not think of one thing—not

one—that she would love better than being snowbound in a little cabin with him.

"I know," she said happily. "I know."

"I don't even know how you get to the cabin in the winter. I'm not canoeing you across the lake in the snow!"

"Joshua?"

"Yes?"

"I trust you to think of something." She paused, and whispered, "I trust you."

"You wouldn't if you knew the perverted thoughts I was having about your toes."

But she saw the words were her gift to him. The one he needed and wanted more than any other. She put her head on his shoulder and found the warmth of his hand.

"I trust you," she whispered again. "With my forever after."

EPILOGUE

JOSHUA COLE stood behind Angel's Rest at Moose Lake Lodge. It was a rare moment alone, and the sounds of summer—a vigorous game of football, laughter, the shouts of children down on the beach— drifted up to him.

He held a rose to plant and a spade, and he looked for the perfect place in the rugged garden that had been started there. Four years had passed since he had first laid eyes on this place, and first acknowledged the stirrings of his own heart.

Four years had not changed much about Moose Lake Lodge. It remained stable while all around it changed.

Dannie had an innate sense for what the world wanted: a family place, a home away from home, a place basically untouched by modern conveniences, by technology, by all those things like TV sets and computers that put distance between people who shared the same homes.

Moose Lake Lodge had become Sun's first family resort. It was not a runaway financial success, but it stood for something way more important than financial success. It was his favorite of all the Sun resorts.

"Susie, Susie Blue-Toes."

His son, Jared, now eleven, was down there torment-
ing his niece, refusing her command to be called Susan
now that she had reached the mature age of eight. His
nephew, Jake, now four, had the same contempt for the
new baby that his sister had once had for him. Sally and
Michael managed the place, their three grandchildren
had come to live here with them since the death of Sally
and Michael's daughter, Darlene, in the spring.

Moose Lake Lodge seemed a natural place for those
children, since they had been able to spend so much
time here with their mother. The only real change Sun
had ever made to the lodge was to make Angel's Rest
completely wheelchair accessible, so that Darlene could
spend her last few summers here.

In the folds of what had become a family.

His son, Jared, and the Morgans, came every year for
the whole summer. Joshua never stopped learning from
the Morgans' generosity of spirit, from how they had
included him in their lives without a moment's pause or
hesitation. From them he had learned that love expanded
to include; if it contracted to exclude it was no longer love.

Melanie and Ryan had fallen in love with Moose
Lake Lodge from their first visit. They were entrenched
in the cabin called Piper's Hollow for every long
weekend and every summer. Susie and Jake acted as if
they owned the whole place.

No one wanted a pool. Or a new wharf. Or jet skis.
No one wanted new furniture or an outdoor bar.

No one who came here wanted anything to change.

This summer was the baby's first year here. Joshua
had worried his daughter, only four months old, was too
young for cold nights and onslaughts of mosquitoes, for
late nights around the campfire, for noisy children all
wanting to hold her. Dannie had laughed at him.

Dannie, who had come into her own in ways he had not even imagined a woman could come into her own: shining with beauty and light, with laughter and compassion. Somehow Dannie was always at the center of all this love, the spokes around which the wheel turned.

As he thought of her, he heard her shout, turned for a moment from the flower bed, to see if he could catch a glimpse of her.

And there she was, hair flying, feet bare, slender and strong, those long legs flashing in the sun, with every kid in the place trying to catch her and wrest that football from her.

Sometimes he wished her curves back. He remembered her lush full figure when he had first met her.

But she said that once a woman had known love, chocolate just didn't do it anymore. Only four months after the baby, she was back to her normal self.

He turned again to the flower garden that Sally had just planted in Darlene's memory and found an empty place in the rich dark soil. He got down on his hands and knees and began to dig, the sounds of shouting and laughter like music in the background.

Every life, he thought, had a period of Camelot in it, a time overflowing with youth and energy, a time that shimmered with creation and abundance and love.

Joshua had experienced that in his boyhood, and thought he'd lost his chance to have it again, for good, when he had given up Jared.

He'd chased it, tried to manufacture its feeling through the Sun resorts.

But in the end Camelot came to those who did not chase it. It came through grace.

Joshua put the rose in the hole he had made in the ground, tenderly patted the dirt back into place around it, sat back on his heels and admired the buds that promised pure white blooms. To get to Camelot, an ordinary man had to become a knight, to ride into the unknown with only one weapon: a brave heart.

A heart that had faith that all would be good in the end, even if there was plenty of evidence to the contrary.

A heart that that knew a man could not always trust circumstances would go his way, but if he was true, he would always be able to trust himself to deal with those circumstances.

In Camelot, there was only one truth. Money did not heal wounds. Nor did possessions. The biggest lie of all was that time did.

No, here in Camelot, Joshua found comfort in the greatest truth of all: love healed all wounds.

When a man's world burned down and there was nothing left, out of the ashes of despair and hurt and fear, love grew roses.

"Dad-O." The voice drifted up the hill, the name his son Jared had chosen to call him. "Are you coming? Our team needs you."

Joshua gave the rose one final pat, got to his feet, looked across the lake to where a little cabin, Love's Rhapsody, waited. It would probably have to wait awhile yet for them to return there, but just looking at it, he remembered.

Chasing Dannie. Kissing her toes until they were both breathless with wanting. Fusing together to create the boundless miracle that was life.

"Dad-O!" Jared had an eleven-year-old's impatience. And he would never say what he really meant. That he was anxious to spend every second he could with his father before summer ended.

"Coming," Joshua called, and went down the creaking

old boardwalk stairs, two at a time, to a world that was beyond anything he could have ever dreamed of for himself. To a world that was better than any man had a right to dream of for himself.

It was a world that had waited for him when he was lost. Sometimes he called it Camelot.

But he knew its real name was Love.

* * * * *

*In honor of our 60th anniversary, Harlequin®
American Romance® is celebrating by featuring an
all-American male each month, all year long with*
MEN MADE IN AMERICA!
*This June, we'll be featuring American men
living in the West.*

Here's a sneak preview of
THE CHIEF RANGER by Rebecca Winters.

*Chief Ranger Vance Rossiter has to confront the
sister of a man who died while under Vance's watch...
and also confront his attraction to her.*

"Chief Ranger Rossiter?" The sight of the woman who'd stepped inside Vance's office brought him to his feet. "I'm Rachel Darrow. Your secretary said I should come right in."

"Please," he said, walking around his desk to shake her hand. At a glance he estimated she was in her midtwenties. Her feminine curves did wonders for the pale blue T-shirt and jeans she was wearing. "Ranger Jarvis informed me there's a young boy with you."

The unfriendly expression in her beautiful green eyes caught him off guard. "Yes," was her clipped reply. "When we arrived in Yosemite the ranger told me I couldn't go anywhere in the park until I talked to you first."

"That's right."

"Knowing you wanted this meeting to be private, he offered to show my nephew around Headquarters."

So this woman was the victim's sister…. "What's his name?"

"Nicky."

The boy who haunted Vance's dreams now had a name. "How old is he?"

"He turned six three weeks ago. Were you the man in charge when my brother and sister-in-law were killed?"

"Yes. To tell you I'm sorry for what happened couldn't begin to convey my feelings."

The woman's gaze didn't flicker. "I won't even try to describe mine. Just tell me one thing. Was their accident preventable?"

"Yes," he answered without hesitation.

"In other words, the people working under you fell asleep on your watch and two lives were snuffed out as a result."

Hearing it put like that, he had to set the record straight. "My staff had nothing to do with it. I, myself, could have prevented the loss of life."

Ms. Darrow's expression hardened. "So you admit culpability."

"Yes. I take full blame."

A look of pain crossed over her features. "You can just stand there and admit it?" Her cry echoed that of his own tortured soul.

"Yes." He sucked in his breath.

"I work for a cruise line. Aboard ship, it's the captain's responsibility to maintain rigid safety regulations. If a disaster like that had happened while he was in charge he would have been relieved of his command and never given another ship again."

Rachel Darrow couldn't know she was preaching to the converted. "If you've come to the park with the intention of bringing a lawsuit against me for negligence, maybe you should." It would only be what he deserved.

"Maybe I will."

In the next instant, she wheeled around and hurried out of his office. Vance could have gone after her, but it would cause a scene, something he was loath to do for a variety of reasons. In the first place, he needed to cool down before he approached her again.

The discovery of the Darrows' frozen bodies had affected every ranger in the park. A little boy had been orphaned—a boy whose aunt was all he had left.

* * * * *

Will Rachel allow Vance to explain—and will she
let him into her heart?
Find out in
THE CHIEF RANGER
Available June 2009
from Harlequin® American Romance®.

Copyright © 2009 by Rebecca Burton

We'll be spotlighting a different series every month
throughout 2009 to celebrate our 60th anniversary.

Look for Harlequin®
American Romance® in June!

Join us for a year-long celebration of the rugged
American male! From cops to cowboys—
Men Made in America has the hero
you've been dreaming about!

Look for

The Chief Ranger

by Rebecca Winters, on sale in June!

---

www.eHarlequin.com   HARBPA09

You're invited to join our Tell Harlequin Reader Panel!

By joining our new reader panel you will:

- Receive Harlequin® books—they are FREE and yours to keep with no obligation to purchase anything!
- Participate in fun online surveys
- Exchange opinions and ideas with women just like you
- Have a say in our new book ideas and help us publish the best in women's fiction

In addition, you will have a chance to win great prizes and receive special gifts!
See Web site for details. Some conditions apply.
Space is limited.

To join, visit us at

www.TellHarlequin.com.

THBPA0108

REQUEST YOUR FREE BOOKS!
2 FREE NOVELS PLUS 2
FREE GIFTS!

From the Heart, For the Heart

YES! Please send me 2 FREE Harlequin® Romance novels and my 2 FREE gifts (gifts are worth about $10). After receiving them, if I don't wish to receive any more books, I can return the shipping statement marked "cancel". If I don't cancel, I will receive 4 brand-new novels every month and be billed just $3.84 per book in the U.S. or $4.24 per book in Canada. That's a savings of at least 15% off the cover price! It's quite a bargain! Shipping and handling is just 25¢ per book*. I understand that accepting the 2 free books and gifts places me under no obligation to buy anything. I can always return a shipment and cancel at any time. Even if I never buy another book, the two free books and gifts are mine to keep forever.

114 HDN EXFM   314 HDN EXFX

Name	(PLEASE PRINT)	
Address		Apt. #
City	State/Prov.	Zip/Postal Code

Signature (if under 18, a parent or guardian must sign)

Mail to the **Harlequin Reader Service:**
IN U.S.A.: P.O. Box 1867, Buffalo, NY 14240-1867
IN CANADA: P.O. Box 609, Fort Erie, Ontario L2A 5X3

Not valid to current subscribers of Harlequin Romance books.

**Are you a subscriber of Harlequin Romance books
and want to receive the larger-print edition?
Call 1-800-873-8635 today!**

* Terms and prices subject to change without notice. Prices do not include applicable taxes. Sales tax applicable in N.Y. Canadian residents will be charged applicable provincial taxes and GST. Offer not valid in Quebec. This offer is limited to one order per household. All orders subject to approval. Credit or debit balances in a customer's account(s) may be offset by any other outstanding balance owed by or to the customer. Please allow 4 to 6 weeks for delivery. Offer available while quantities last.

Your Privacy: Harlequin Books is committed to protecting your privacy. Our Privacy Policy is available online at www.eHarlequin.com or upon request from the Reader Service. From time to time we make our lists of customers available to reputable third parties who may have a product or service of interest to you. If you would prefer we not share your name and address, please check here. ☐

HR09

HARLEQUIN® *Romance*®

Escape Around the World
Dream destinations, whirlwind weddings!

Honeymoon with the Boss
by
JESSICA HART

Top tycoon Tom Maddison is used to calling the shots—until his convenient marriage falls through. But rather than waste his honeymoon, he'll take his boardroom to the beach and bring his oh-so-sensible secretary Imogen on a tropical business trip! But will Tom finally see the sexy woman that prudent Imogen truly is?

Available in June wherever books are sold.

www.eHarlequin.com

HR175900

Coming Next Month

Available June 9, 2009

Travel to tropical shores with the start of our brand-new miniseries
Escape Around the World, and don't miss the final installment
in the *www.blinddatebrides.com* trilogy!

#4099 OUTBACK HEIRESS, SURPRISE PROPOSAL Margaret Way
After inheriting half of her grandfather's empire, Francesca must fight
the reignition of old flames when she discovers the joint heir is her
childhood sweetheart, Bryn....

#4100 HONEYMOON WITH THE BOSS Jessica Hart
Escape Around the World
When Imogen's boss's marriage of convenience falls through, the
honeymoon becomes a tropical business trip! But will Tom finally see the
sexy woman beneath his sensible PA?

#4101 HIS PRINCESS IN THE MAKING Melissa James
Toby has always secretly loved his best friend, Lia. But when Lia
discovers she's *Suddenly Royal!* and a princess, Toby must compete
with an entire kingdom for her attention!

#4102 DREAM DATE WITH THE MILLIONAIRE Melissa McClone
When *www.blinddatebrides.com* pairs her with gorgeous millionaire
Bryce, bombshell Dani knows he will judge her poor background like
every man does. But Bryce isn't just any man!

#4103 MAID IN MONTANA Susan Meier
In Her Shoes...
Though she is nothing like the glamorous women who inhabit Jeb's
world, housekeeper and single mom Sophie wishes she could be more
than just Jeb's maid in Montana!

#4104 HIRED: THE ITALIAN'S BRIDE Donna Alward
Heart to Heart
Mariella is determined not to let her new boss Luca's laid-back attitude
ruin her hard work. But she soon discovers Luca could be the very
person to help her overcome her dark past....

HRCNMBPA0509